✦ TELLING ✦

✦ TELLING ✦

CAROL MATAS

KEY PORTER BOOKS

Canadian Cataloguing in Publication Data

Matas, Carol, 1949–
    Telling

ISBN 1-55013-933-9

I. Title.

PS8576.A7994T44 1988   jC813'.54   C97-932447-5
PZ7.M37Te 1998

Poems
Page 35: "I wait" © 1997 Rebecca Brask; 63: "Reality's house" © 1997 Rebecca
Brask; 89: "Two" © 1997 Rebecca Brask; 109: "Roots" © 1997 Rebecca Brask;
117: "Here I go" and "Lover, again" © 1997 Sarah Kobrinsky

The publisher gratefully acknowledges
the assistance of the Canada Council and
the Ontario Arts Council.

THE CANADA COUNCIL   LE CONSEIL DES ARTS
FOR THE ARTS   DU CANADA
SINCE 1957   DEPUIS 1957

Key Porter Books Limited
70 The Esplanade
Toronto, Ontario
Canada M5E 1R2

Printed and bound in Canada

98 99 00 01 6 5 4 3 2 1

For Maria
who knows what it's like . . .

Acknowledgments

Thanks to Rebecca Brask and Sarah Kobrinsky who wrote the poems found in this book when they were the same age as Sue, seventeen. And to Perry Nodelman for his critiques, and to my editor Barbara Berson.

PROLOGUE

This is a story about stories—about me, and my sisters, and what we tell each other. I guess it's also about what we don't tell and why we've done what we've done. Mom always says "That's a slice," meaning that's a slice of life. Well, here's a slice of ours—the summer that's half over and me with an uncontrollable urge to tell about it. . . .

CHAPTER 1

Lightning crackled outside the second-story window. It's true, it really did! Okay, so my English teacher, Mrs. Mills, told me never to start a story with the weather, but I think rules are made to be broken. I mean, should I leave out the storm because it's too corny, even if it really happened? No way!

> *The weird sisters, hand in hand,*
> *Posters of the sea and land,*
> *Thus do go about, about.*

My sisters and I whispered the chant as we held hands and circled around and around. We went faster and faster, the chant quickened until a crack of thunder shook the house, and we fell to the floor, giggling and laughing.

"Shh," warned Sue, "we'll wake Mom." Sue was *always* that way about Mom. Mommy's little helper.

"Yeah, right," I replied, "as if the thunder isn't four million times as loud as we are." Not that I didn't care about Mom. Just that I thought Sue always went overboard.

Sue pushed herself up, climbed into the bed and settled herself with two pillows behind her back.

"Tell all," she commanded.

Sue also tended to be a bit bossy—being the oldest and all.

"Pillows!" cried Corey as she scrambled off the floor and raced out the door.

"Bring mine," I called, taking advantage of Corey's absence to settle in at the end of the bed, back against the wall.

Corey squealed, "No fair," throwing the pillows at me when she returned. "I always get the floor."

"That," said Sue, "is because you are the youngest, will always be the youngest, and will always get the floor. When we're forty and doing this you'll still get the floor."

"Well, I hope that by *then* you'll have a room with a decent chair in it," Corey grumbled, "oh, brilliant eldest of us all, who'd better make lots of money so she can take care of her youngest sister who will be a poor starving actress in a hovel somewhere in New York."

We were in Sue's room, on the second floor of our house. We live near the downtown area, which consists mostly of big old wood-frame houses, wide streets, lots of trees. According to Mom, she and Dad bought the house for a song when Sue was a baby and spent years sanding the wood, painting, fixing. Mom once said that after they'd finished creating together—us three sisters and the house—they found they had no other common interests. Dad got into building and construction in a big way. When they asked him to go supervise a new condo development in Vancouver he took the job, but neglected to take his family. He sends a big cheque every once in a while, but he's remarried and he doesn't really keep in touch. Sometimes we (my sisters and I, not my mom) think of surprising him with a visit but basically we figure if he couldn't care less about us why should we care about him? We try not to think about him too much.

Anyway, our house has a screened-in porch—excellent when the mosquitoes descend on us—and huge front and back yards which are fierce to mow in summer and even worse to get the leaves off in the fall. There are three bedrooms and a bathroom upstairs, and downstairs there's a huge kitchen, small dining room, big living room and an extra room which Mom turned into a bedroom. She works such unpredictable hours as a nurse and midwife she prefers to be away from the noise of our blasters and be more on her own. Because Sue is the oldest she got the room meant to be the master bedroom. She painted it off-white, and over the years has collected Mexican artefacts and Aboriginal art so her room looks like a little bit of New Mexico (I guess—I've never been there). Sue herself is tallish with blond hair and blue eyes, high cheekbones, a classic beauty.

Corey and I have small rooms. Corey's is as messy as Sue's is neat. I mean, Sue even makes her bed before she goes to school. Corey, on the other hand, has probably *never* made her bed. Her room does have a chest of drawers but she refuses to use it. She dumps all her clean laundry on the floor along with her dirty laundry, but she swears she knows which is which, and she and her friends stomp on it all indiscriminately. She has her pale pink walls covered in posters of rock stars and magazine ads. She refuses to have a desk as that would take up too much room so she does all her homework sitting on her bed. As to Corey's looks—she's very short, only five four or something, with brown hair and brown eyes—that is, it was brown till she dyed it auburn at the beginning of the summer.

I'm somewhere in between Sue and Corey. Which is no surprise, I guess, being the middle sister. My room is not spotless, but I do use my drawers. I've painted it a deep forest green, I love that colour, and I have posters of Magic Johnson and Michael Jordan and Nirvana and Bob Dylan up. You may wonder about Bob Dylan but Martha (my best friend) and I love him. Mom was playing him one day and what great songs he does! As for my looks—I'm six feet with chestnut hair, thick and wavy (chestnut is deep rich brown, I *never* describe my hair as brown, *ugh*!) and I have green eyes and in the summer I freckle (double ugh).

Sue plumped her pillows.

"Corey, you didn't shut the door."

"I'm not getting up again. You shut the door."

"You're closer."

I sighed, got off the bed and shut the door.

"The middle child," I quipped, "is always the best adjusted, *and* the happiest."

The rain began to pelt the windows. While I was up I turned out the light and made sure the blinds over the window opposite the bed were up all the way. Corey got off the floor and squeezed in, back against the wall in the middle of Sue and me. The lightning flashed, both sheet and fork.

"Speak, children," Sue commanded once again. "Tell your sister all."

Sue always said something like that when we began our "Tellings." That's what we call it when we get together to tell what's been happening to us. Mom encouraged Sue to get us younger ones to talk to her—to Sue, that is—if Mom was away, which she often was, and is, working. Being a single parent in a low-paid job like a nurse isn't easy—Mom works twelve-hour shifts, three weeks on days, three weeks on nights. When she works nights she's around all day, driving us crazy. When she works days she's never around, and that drives us crazy too. We had to learn to depend on each other. So after a while it became a habit, late at night, all of us confiding in one another. And we'd added the formal aspect of the chant as well, to begin and end our sessions.

"Why don't *you* tell first," I said. "We *always* go first. I want to hear all about Patti's dad's house. Was it huge? Like, were the telephones gold? What?"

"How I spent my summer vacation, by Sue Erikson. Sick of working at McDonald's, camp-counsellor job not starting till August, Sue accepted an invitation from her friend Patti to go visit Patti's dad in Toronto, for one month. Thought it would make a change and it did."

"What did you do?" I said.

"Nothing."

"Nothing?"

"Well, we hung around the pool all day mostly. Patti's dad took us to a ball game once and to Stratford once. . . ."

"Where you saw *Macbeth*!" Corey exclaimed.

"Right. Funny it should be that play, isn't it?" Sue smiled. "Anyway, there really isn't much to tell."

Sue has a way of hiding her feelings by making her face go kinda blank. That's what she did then. I knew she was hiding something and so did Corey, who said, "There's more there than you're telling."

"Maybe. But you guys tell first. Corey?"

"No, Alex goes first."

"Alex?"

"Well, okay. I'll go first." Actually, I'd been dying to talk and although I tried to sound reluctant I really wasn't. "I'll start with my first day at work—the day after you left. It was weird. I mean, like, the night before, everyone had been cheering me and I was this big star—"

"Swelled head, swelled head," Corey interrupted.

"Well, I *was* a big star. Our team had won and the girls had carried me around the gym in this victory march and everyone in the stands had been screaming and clapping. You should've been there," I said to Sue, still angry with her for leaving before the big game. "Anyway, I went from being this big basketball star to being just another kid in the gym, first day at work for the Renaissance Fair. This guy Gordon, he's around forty or so, he's our boss and he called out the names and split us into groups. So guess who's in my group? None other than Ms. Popularity herself, Chelsea Mills. She's *so* perfect, all that blond hair and those blue eyes and the Barbie-doll figure. And there's this guy Dan. . . ."

"Ooooh, Dan!" Corey cooed. She has *never* learned not to interrupt.

"Shut up!" I snapped at her.

"Is he hot?" Sue asked.

"Yeah, he's hot. He's actually *taller* than me, like he must be six foot four, black wavy hair down to his shoulders, earring, built—"

"Enough!" Sue exclaimed. "I can hardly stand it."

"Oh, yeah," I added, "and he's got green eyes just like me."

"Oh my God, no," Sue exhaled. "So? So?"

"So nothing." If Sue was going to hide stuff, then so could I.

"Don't listen to her," Corey said, "*nothing* isn't quite the right word."

"Am I telling this or not?" I said, glaring at Corey.

"Tell, tell," Sue urged.

"So there was Chelsea, Dan—"

"The beautiful people," grinned Sue.

"Right, the beautiful people. Then Chelsea's buddy Lee-Ann, sort of a Chelsea clone but not quite as perfect, and last but not least, Paul."

"The number-one nerd of the universe," Corey interrupted again.

"That's what I thought too, at first," I agreed. "His pants are like, pressed or something, and he wears these button-down shirts and cardigans. Sort of a young Mr. Rogers. And his hair is really short, you know? Anyway that was our group. Gordon told us we had to create a fifteen-minute play to perform every couple hours at the Renaissance Fair, plus we'd each be given a character and a costume and we'd be expected to walk around the fair in costume." I grinned at Sue. "So anyway, guess what character I was given?"

Sue shrugged. "No idea."

"A witch!"

"Really?"

"Yes, really. And that's how all the trouble started."

"Trouble?"

"Man, you could say so," Corey quipped. "Trouble she got *herself* into."

"Oh, and you're one to talk, little Miss I-do-everything-my-friends-do," I shot back.

"Shut up."

"What's all this?" Sue asked.

"Never mind," Corey grumbled.

"You'll have to tell," I warned her.

"No, I won't," Corey grimaced. "You can't *make* me."

"Then you can't be here when I tell," I said.

"I'm not leaving."

"Yes, you are."

Sue intervened. "You're staying, Corey. *And* you're telling. That's the deal. That's the pact."

Corey sighed. "Fine."

Sue turned back to me.

"I want to hear all about 'the trouble,'" Sue stated. "Beginning to end. The way we always tell it. Secret thoughts included."

"It'll take a while," I warned.

"Are we going anywhere?" Sue said. "Go. And remember the rules," she warned Corey. "*No* talking, *no* interrupting, Alex tells her story *her* way."

CHAPTER 2

Before I continue with what happened that night let me describe the fair.

Each year our little city hosts a huge Renaissance Fair. The fairground is on the northwest outskirts of town and takes up at least two acres. It's built to have the look of medieval or Renaissance Europe, with shop façades built to the time, actors dressed in Renaissance costume and old-fashioned entertainments. The rides for kids, for instance, use no electricity and are called things like the Carousello, the Butterfly ride or the Hippogriff. There are lots of craftspeople who exhibit their wares, roving minstrel bands, picnic tables to eat at (there is every food imaginable); games like ball toss, the king's stockade, spinner darts, crossbows or king-of-the-log; fortune-telling, demonstrations of artwork like glass blowing or pottery making—it is just an amazing place. Mom has taken us since we were little and I've *always* wanted to work there. *Always*. Finally this year I got accepted because they decided to allow a group of fourteen- and fifteen-year-olds to work on a trial basis. Normally you have to be sixteen. We had to have top marks in school and be model workers since they were just testing the idea of hiring younger kids. If we messed up they wouldn't hire young kids again next year. Big responsibility. That definitely affected my decisions—not always in the right way—but I *was* under a lot of pressure.

"I actually thought it would be kinda neat to be a witch," I began. "Paul was a peasant, Dan a priest. And I figured I was used to being a witch from all the playing we do with it, so I was excited.

"'The play's easy,' Dan said. 'We'll do a witch-burning.'

"'But,' Chelsea objected, 'that's not fair. Then Alex gets to play the lead. What can a lady do in a witch-burning?'

"I realized that she was right. Dan, who didn't even know me, had just handed me the lead. I wasn't going to let it slip away, so I had to think of something to calm Chelsea down.

"'Well, of course the witch will say she's innocent. And she'll come to you so you can try to save her. And the lady-in-waiting can be like the witch's friend or something. Before she found out she was a witch.'

"'And the priest will conduct the trial, of course,' said Dan.

"'And what about me?' Paul asked, in this really quiet voice.

"We all looked at Paul. What was there for a peasant to do?

"'I could be married to the witch,' Paul suggested. 'And not know she's a witch.'

"I *hated* that idea, so I really had to think fast.

"'How about if you're the one that accuses me?' I suggested. 'Like I mean, maybe something happened to your crop, and you saw me looking at you funny one day and you figured I'd cast a spell on you.'

"'That's terrific!' Dan applauded.

"Paul looked disappointed, but was I relieved. Married to him? Ugh. And he'd probably try to figure out a way so we'd have to kiss. The only way he could get a girl to kiss him, no doubt.

"I glanced at Dan. He obviously had no such problems. He grinned at me and gave me a little wink.

"At that point Gordon came round and suggested that we all head over to the library to do a little research on witches and the Inquisition and witch-burnings if that was what our play was going to be about. So we walked over as a group, but it was really Chelsea and Lee-Ann together, me and Dan together, and then Paul sort of trailing behind.

"Dan asked me why we'd never met. I told him I had no idea. 'I mean, I know we go to different high schools but still,' he said, 'it's such a small place. What's your last name?'

"'Erikson,' I told him.

"'Oh,' he said, 'fine Nordic blood, right? Norwegian?'

"I nodded.

"'Me too,' he laughed.

"I glanced at his black hair.

"'Actually my dad's Norwegian, my mom's Italian. I got her hair. But my little sister is blond.' He eyed my hair.

"'I confess,' I said, 'the chestnut colour is from my mom's side. There's a Scot in there somewhere.'

"'Hey,' he said, 'you're not *the* Alex Erikson. The basketball star?'

"I must've turned bright red. 'I guess.'

"'Everyone at Pearson High *hates* you. We were sure we were gonna win the championship this year, but I heard you barrelled over our entire team.'

"I couldn't tell whether he was saying it as a compliment or if he didn't approve.

"'That's how you play the game,' I said. 'Isn't it?'

"'Yeah, I guess,' he said, and I still couldn't tell what he was thinking.

"'You ever play?' I said.

"He shook his head. 'So it's your mom that's involved in that court case then?'

"'Oh, great, I thought, does the *entire* world know? I mean, just when you think everyone's forgotten about it. . . . And like I *know* that was one of the reasons you went away, Sue."

Sue didn't disagree. No point. She knew I'd guessed the real reason for her wanting to get away.

"And *I* know Mom was right and everything, but here I am meeting this incredibly cool guy and we end up talking about Mom. So I told him that Mom has done lots of home births and this is the first one that anything had gone wrong on and that even had it happened in the hospital they *almost* for sure would have lost the baby anyway, and that it wasn't the parents who were suing Mom, it was the doctors' federation

22

who want midwives out of their business 'cause it costs them lots of lost money.

"I don't know. Like, he didn't say much there either and I was starting to wonder if he was just quiet, or whether he disapproved of me in some way or other. It was strange. But you know me, I never, or I try not to ever, let what other people think bother me and so I just ignored it and when we got to the library I got to work. He *did* tell me that his dad is a doctor, so maybe his dad told him all sorts of nasty stuff about midwives, who knows.

"Anyway, it was what happened at the library that *really* started all the trouble. I found this novel all about the witch-burnings in the 1600s in France. And I came home that night and read it in one go. And you know what I found out? Most of the women who were burned as witches weren't practising witchcraft at all. They were just women, most of them without husbands to protect them, who were accused by neighbours or by the Church Inquisition or by a judge. But you know what's really amazing? The other big group of women who were persecuted were midwives!"

"Really?" Sue interrupted, forgetting her vow of silence.

"You said *no* talking," Corey accused.

"Ooops, sorry," Sue said, hand over mouth.

"Midwives," I continued. "And healers. Sound a little familiar? Their biggest enemies were male doctors who were just starting to go to schools and wanted women out of their way so they could hog the market. Women healers knew a *lot* back then. They knew all about herbs and flowers and making potions that really worked. I mean, doctors are finding out now that some of this stuff actually works—and it certainly didn't *hurt*, anyway, whereas the male doctors were cutting people up and bleeding them with leeches. The next day I got more material to read—and like, a lot of the priests then were *really* sick. They were terrified of all this devil-worship stuff and I guess repressed, 'cause they couldn't have sex, so they fantasized that these women were having these orgies with the devil and stealing the local men's 'members,' shrinking them, then keeping them in boxes wriggling around!"

At this point, despite their vow of silence, which they hadn't really kept anyway, both Sue and Corey broke up screaming with laughter. Sue almost fell off the bed.

"No, no, not true," she squealed. "You're making it up!"

"I'm not!" I protested. "And *you* are interrupting."

Sue tried to stop laughing but the more she tried the more she giggled, which became contagious, and pretty soon all of us were shrieking and repeating words like "wiggling around," "all shrunk," which would set us off again.

"Girls, some of us have to work in the morning!" came Mom's angry voice from her bedroom.

"Sorry!" we screamed in unison.

"Water," Sue gasped, "I need water."

"I'm hungry," Corey added.

"Mini-break," I declared, "for water and taco chips."

We raced down the stairs to the kitchen to gather large glasses of water, chips, and a bowl of hot sauce and then we tiptoed quietly back up, shut the door and settled on the floor around the food. I turned on the desk reading lamp for some dim light, as the lightning seemed to be dying down.

"Go on, Alex," Sue said, "this is all a weird coincidence."

"Well, I was pretty blown away by all this," I continued, "Especially considering Mom. I mean it seemed like the witch-burning had a lot more to do with women being *women* than being witches. So I went into rehearsal the next day and laid all this out to the group. What was their response, you might ask? Chelsea let me know right away.

"'Who cares? It's boring,' she said.

"'Like *really* boring,' Lee-Ann added.

"'So what's your *point*, exactly?' Dan said.

"And Paul didn't say anything. As if he knew no one cared what he thought.

"'My point is I don't want to be a witch any more,' I declared. 'I want to be a woman healer who is *accused* of being a witch, but is just an innocent woman. You guys have *got* to read this book.'

"Then Dan smiled at me. This gorgeous smile.

"'It's a perfect play the way we have it now, Alex,' he said, gazing into my eyes. 'The woman is a witch. She curses people and brews potions. She's put on trial, but first runs to her friend and the lady of the manor and pleads with them to save her. We have a short trial and a mock burning and the crowd goes home happy. I mean it could be hard to make it too complicated. It isn't supposed to be serious. We only have fifteen minutes.'

"'And remember,' Chelsea added, 'the fair hired you to be a witch. You're getting a witch's costume. Not a healer's costume.'" I tried to mimic the sarcastic drip to her voice, but only Chelsea can really get it perfect. "'So do you want to go against the fair? They'd probably fire you. And the rest of the group hates the idea so you'd better drop it—now.'

"'But,' I protested, 'what we're doing isn't *real*. I mean it wasn't what *really* happened.'

"'It's what everyone *thinks* happened,' Lee-Ann chirped in. 'That's all that matters, right?'

"'Excuse me,' and now Paul was going to pipe up with something no one wanted to hear, 'but I think Alex has a point. Shouldn't we be historically accurate?'

"'We are!' exclaimed Chelsea. 'As far as everyone knows.'

"'Yes,' Paul continued doggedly, 'but *we* know it isn't true. Alex has done some research and found some little-known facts. Men have written history from their perspective. And *they* thought women healers and midwives were witches. I went to the library too, and I couldn't find any first-hand accounts of the witch trials written by women—it was all written by their prosecutors, the men.'

"'Well, of course you couldn't, Dodo Brain,' Dan laughed. 'It's hard to write an account of your trial when you've just been burned at the stake.'

"'But,' continued Paul, 'they could have written their own stories before they died—or told them to a scribe, because most women couldn't read or write.'

"By this time everyone was laughing at Paul, who sounded

like a teacher, and I was feeling like an idiot. I knew I was right but I started to buckle when Dan went after the idea, and when Paul took my side—well, I didn't want him to! I wanted Dan to!

"'You're right,' I said to the group, glaring at Paul, who stared at his feet and got a look like a wet puppy. That made me even madder! 'I'll just be a witch. Who needs the hassle?' I really didn't want to create any trouble.

"'That's a nice girl,' Dan said and he winked at me. 'You were almost turning into a witch yourself there for a minute.'

"I smiled back at him, but I felt really funny inside. I *wanted* to be nice, I didn't *want* to create trouble, but why was sticking up for myself considered making trouble? It was so different than on the courts. I mean, there I get my way 'cause I'm fast and I'm aggressive. No one wants me to be nice. Why was this so different?"

CHAPTER 3

I had asked a question that neither of my sisters seemed to be able to answer. Neither offered me any advice—I guess they were just waiting to hear how the story turned out, to see if I'd figured it out for myself. They thought the question was what Mom would call a rhetorical question, one not really demanding an answer. So I just continued my story.

"We started to write the play," I said. And then it occurred to me that my sisters couldn't understand unless they read the play, so I made a suggestion.

"You guys want to read it?" I asked.

"Oh, yeah," Corey retorted, "that would be *lots* of fun."

Sometimes I just feel like *shaking* her!

"*I'd* like to," Sue offered.

Corey grunted. "Great."

"All right," I said, "let's read it together. That way no one has to sit around waiting while the other person reads it."

Corey moaned, but two overruled one so she had to agree. I must admit the more she objected the more I enjoyed making her do it. She's so insensitive. At least she could've pretended to be interested.

I ran to my room and came back with the script. I handed it to Sue. "You two can share," I suggested, "and read the others' parts. I'll do my part."

"How long did it take you to write this, Alex?" Sue asked as she looked it over.

"About a week," I replied. "The bad thing was that every time I tried to squeeze in something more historically accurate Dan would sidle up and wink at me or tease me till I quit."

"And what was happening *during* that week?" Corey prodded. "Let's not leave anything out."

Corey was *so* annoying!

"I was going out with Dan. Big deal."

"Every night!" Corey exclaimed.

"And what were *you* doing every night? Your turn for a while, Corey. Let's hear what you were up to."

Corey's attitude was really bugging me. She was needling me, but I knew she had nothing to feel so superior about. Also I really wanted Sue to hear what Corey had been up to. Maybe Sue could knock some sense into her. I figured the script could wait for a few minutes.

"Fine, we'll take a little break," Sue agreed. "Corey, you tell us what you were up to. Just that week."

"Yeah, Corey, tell us what *you* were doing," I echoed.

"I was just hanging out with my friends," Corey said defiantly. "You know, my friends. Anything wrong with that?"

"Oh, and what about running away two days after Sue left on holidays?" I said, jumping in. Now, you have to understand, I wasn't "telling" on her. Our pact was that we were supposed to tell everything, and she wasn't.

"You ran away?" Sue asked. She looked really shocked.

"Not really."

"Well, what then?"

"I just ran out of the house 'cause I was mad at Mom."

"Why?" Sue looked *very sceptical and* Corey kind of squirmed.

"All my friends have an eleven o'clock curfew. Mom insists I have to be home by ten! It's ridiculous! So I just stayed out till I wanted to. My friends think I'm a baby."

"Why do you care *what* they think?" I accused.

"Man, that's funny coming from *you*."

"I've never been part of a mob like you. I've got one good friend, Martha, and a few other pals and that's it. I've *never* travelled in a mob. I've *always* done my own thing."

"Yeah, like with the play, right? You're this big feminist, equal to any guy, but the minute one makes googly eyes at you it's 'Yes, Dan, of course, Dan, anything *you* say, Dan.'"

"I'm *not* a feminist," I shouted at her.

"What's wrong with being a feminist?" Sue wondered aloud.

"I don't need all that," I protested. "I'm as good as any guy and I don't need any special treatment!"

"Shhh," Sue hissed. "What's the matter with you! Chill out. Methinks the lady doth protest too much."

Now that I think about it I wonder how *feminist* became such a dirty word for my age group. Mom is proud to be called a feminist. But, at school, guys use it like a bad word. Girls do too, like if you're ugly or too intense. I personally think it's a reaction against women becoming powerful. Or that's what I think *now*, after this summer. It's like a dirty word to call someone when they aren't being "nice." But I'm getting ahead of myself. Sue was determined to get the truth from Corey.

"All right, little sister," Sue said sternly, "what is this about running away?"

"I stayed out till midnight, that's all."

"And you came home drunk!" I added.

"Everyone was drinking. I just had a couple beers."

"Where did you get beers at your age?" Sue said.

"I'm thirteen. I'm in grade eight. Some of the kids in my class are doing it already. You don't think I can drink a beer?"

"Did you like it?" Sue asked.

"Yes," Corey replied defiantly. "I loved it."

"Do you like the smoking, too?" I asked.

"Yes!"

"Corey!" Sue exclaimed. "You aren't smoking! That's so stupid!"

"I've seen *you* smoke," Corey shot back.

"Because *I've* been dumb you have to be dumb too? I quit 'cause I smelled horrible all the time, like an old ashtray, and I had this constant cough."

"The tobacco companies are killing you and laughing while they take your money—getting you to pay them for it!" I exclaimed.

"Oh, shut up, Alex!" Corey spat out. "I'm sick of your lectures. You're not so perfect."

"What did Mom do?" Sue asked.

"She grounded me."

"For how long?"

"All week."

"So you got to stay in all week instead of having to be home at ten," Sue said. "The point?"

"It's cooler to be grounded than to have to be home at ten like some baby."

Sue sighed. "Is there more?" she asked.

"Yeah," Corey admitted, "but that's everything that happened the first week. Which is all Alex told."

"You're just postponing," Sue said, shaking her head. "You'll have to tell the rest. Get it over with. Tell it now."

"No!" Then Corey obviously figured a way out—she's very good at that. "You haven't told us about your week one."

Corey couldn't have cared less right at that moment about Sue's week. She just wanted Sue off her back. I wasn't going to let Corey get away with it, until Sue said, "I told you there's nothing to tell!"

Then I *knew* Sue was hiding something, so I got really curious.

"Nothing to tell, huh? What about Mark?" I said casually. I was fishing, really.

"Mark? Who told you about Mark?"

Her face flushed. I knew I was on to something.

"Patti," I said.

"When did you talk to Patti?"

"She called when you were at the store with Mom, remember?"

"What did she say?"

"She asked if Mark had called here yet. And I asked her who Mark was and she said, 'Oh, no one, just a boy.' So if he's no one why would he be calling here?"

"Had he called her house?" Sue asked.

"She didn't say."

"Did she say anything else?"

"No."

Sue sat silent, offering no explanation.

"Tell!" I demanded. I was dying to know.

"Tell!" Corey agreed.

"You have to," I said. "We have. We still are. There's lots more to tell. I won't if you won't."

"It's still your turn," Sue protested.

"The first week," I insisted, with no intention of letting her squirm out of this one. "We did."

"The first week?"

"Yes."

Since Sue has always taken the role of "other Mom" it's hard to get her to confide in her younger sisters. It's partly habit. We *were* too young to understand a lot until recently. But now it's different. It should become more equal between us. The trouble is, Sue is *very* quiet, you see. Very—restrained. She doesn't talk a lot. Doesn't show a lot of emotion. The exact opposite of Corey, in fact! But she writes poetry. And she kind of leaves it around for us to read. Corey never bothers but I always read it, because it tells more about what is going on inside Sue than she ever will. I mean, she'll tell you events, what happens, the action, you know. But not the inside *feelings*.

Placing my pen on the white lined paper,
I wait
for my world to appear.
Praying for my endless thoughts
to wash out my mind.
So I sit,
with my pen and my paper
and wait.

She wrote that after she got back from Toronto, so I knew *something* was up. Her version was *very* short.

"We got there and I was given my own room with its own bath on the second floor. I thought Patti's dad would be a rich snob, but he was really nice. Her stepmom *is* a real snob, but—hey. I mean she spends her entire day shopping and getting her hair done and her nails done. Like one of those dingbats in the movies. She took us shopping every day that first week, which was great fun for me since, of course, I had no money. She spent a fortune on Patti and she bought me some stuff too even though I kept telling her not to. She said it was no fun if someone was left out, so, well, I showed you that skirt and top."

"It's gorgeous," Corey sighed. "I'm so glad you gave in and didn't stick to your stupid principles!"

"My principles aren't stupid," Sue objected. Then she paused before she added, "But I guess I'm sick of them, a bit. Being Mom's perfect little girl, always doing the right thing, helping at the women's clinic, all that stuff. After I gave in I have to admit I kinda enjoyed myself."

I was glad to hear Sue talk about breaking away a bit from Mom. In a weird way she's become our second Mom, so she never just has fun—like kid fun. Maybe now that Corey and me are older she feels she can think a bit more about herself.

"And Mark?" Corey asked.

"He's in first year at University of Toronto and he plays bass guitar in a band. But I didn't meet him till week two, so I don't have to tell yet."

"That's not fair!" Corey exclaimed.

"Alex said week one. That's all," Sue replied calmly. "And that's what I just told you. Now let's read the play. I want to see how it turned out."

She was right, technically, and besides I did want her to hear my play. At least now I knew who Mark was.

"This is the first version," I said.

"There's another?" Sue asked.

"That's part of what's still to tell."

Corey read the parts of the Servant and the Priest. Sue

read the Lady and the Peasant. And, of course, I was the Witch. Sue is an awful reader, by the way, no expression. Corey, on the other hand, although she didn't want to do it at first, really got going. She was *good*. Maybe she will be an actress someday.

CHAPTER 4

THE BURNING
(A short play for the Renaissance Fair)

(Witch has hand out to Peasant)

PEASANT: Go away now, Madame Lorie, I have nothing to give you.

WITCH: No coin? No small bit of grain or even a vegetable? Not even a little turnip?

PEASANT: Nothing! I gave to you just a week ago. Now leave me be!

WITCH: You'll be sorry, Master Lipcott. God punishes those who do not follow His way and his Son's way. You'll be sorry!!

(Both exit, then Peasant re-enters with Priest)

PEASANT: I tell you, my entire crop has a blight and it was only weeks ago that Madame Lorie cursed me. She said God would punish me. But it isn't God who's doing the punishing. I've always been a good Christian, you know that, Father. It's the Devil—that woman is in league with the Devil!

PRIEST: This is a very serious accusation, Master Lipcott.

PEASANT: Can there be any other explanation?

PRIEST: Now that you mention it, there was the terrible business of poor little Suzanne who died so suddenly just last week.

PEASANT: And my neighbours the Salins? Their cow went dry just yesterday. And the witch had been there that morning!

PRIEST: I will post a notice in the town square—any that feel she has harmed them must come forward. (*Exit*)

(*Enter* Witch *and* Servant)

WITCH: Please, Anne, you must let me see your mistress!

SERVANT: She's very busy today.

WITCH: I need her help. They are accusing me of being a witch!

(*Enter* Lady)

LADY: What is all this racket?

SERVANT: I'm sorry, my lady, but Madame Lorie wants to speak with you.

LADY: Well, what is it then?

WITCH: Please my lady, they are accusing me of being a witch. I need your help.

LADY: And just why should I help you?

WITCH: Because you are so good. They will make me suffer.

LADY: No more than you deserve, if you have made them suffer!

WITCH: (*Pointing her finger at* Lady) I will curse you as well if you do not help me. You have two children. I can brew a potion, say a prayer and they will die, suddenly, like little Suzanne. I warn you, you *will* help me!!

SERVANT: Get out, you hag! We aren't afraid of you!

LADY: Don't hurt my children. Promise you won't hurt my children.

WITCH: Promise you will help me.

LADY: Yes, I promise, I promise.

SERVANT: My lady!

LADY: Quiet! (*to* Witch) Now leave us!

(*Exit* Witch)

LADY: We must speak to the priest. This woman must be stopped. And quickly. For the meantime she must think we are her friends or my children are in danger.

SERVANT: Yes, of course, my lady, of course you're right.

(*Exit both. Enter* Priest, *then* Lady)

LADY: Father, you must help me!

PRIEST: Of course, my lady. What is it?

LADY: That dreadful woman, Madame Lorie, threatened to put a curse on my children.

PRIEST: Then she will be brought to trial. And it must be

41

done quickly, before she inflicts any more suf-
fering on my poor people.

LADY: Thank you, Father.

(They walk back toward the rear of the stage, as
Peasant, Servant *and* Witch *enter.* Witch *sits on*
chair centre stage. Priest *stands,* Peasant *sits on*
floor stage left, Lady *and* Servant *sit on chair stage*
right)

PRIEST: You must confess so that you can go to heaven
pure. Otherwise, the Devil will surely take you.

WITCH: But I am just a poor widow with not two coins
to rub together. Everyone is after me because
they are too stingy to help me!

PEASANT: I accuse you of putting a curse on my crops.

LADY: And I accuse you of threatening the lives of my
children!

WITCH: *(Glares at* Lady) You said you would help me!

LADY: This evil must stop!

WITCH: *(Pointing finger at* Lady) And now I do curse you
and your children. You will die slow deaths and
painful, you will suffer. . . .

(Lady screams and faints. Servant *rushes to tend*
her)

PRIEST: Stop! *(Holds up Bible)* The Lord will win over
your curses. This is all the proof I need. You
will die today, for today I pronounce you a
witch, servant of your Lord the Devil!

(Witch *is pulled offstage screaming and cursing.*
Lady *awakens*)

LADY: My children! She cursed them!

SERVANT: No, my lady. The good father interrupted her
            before she could complete her dreadful curse.
            Soon she will be dead. And we will be safe.

LADY: It's too terrible to think that she has been living
            amongst us all this time. I wonder if there are
            others like her as well?

SERVANT: Oh, my lady, do not frighten me so! Quick let us
            hurry home to the poor innocent babies.

LADY: Yes, let us.

(*We hear the scream of the* Witch)

PEASANT
& PRIEST: (*Offstage*) Burn, Witch! Burn!

END

"Well," said Sue, "I can certainly understand why you
don't think this is written the way you'd like it. Did you do
your own lines?"

"I had to, didn't I?" I responded, pulling a face. "I mean,
that's what I was hired to do."

"So what's all this about trouble?"

"It took us a week to write," I explained, "and a week to

rehearse. The fair opened exactly two weeks after we started. And all this time I felt bad—like I wasn't sticking to my principles. So I decided on a little surprise. We did the show four times the first day and it did go over really well. And the rest of the day we walked around in costume and interacted with the crowd. That was kinda fun."

"What's your costume like? Pointy hat, typical witch stuff?" Sue asked.

"No, not really. More the way they'd dress then. Like a hag. Black, ragged, a black hat, but not pointed."

"Well, did you cackle and run around behaving like a witch or not?" Sue asked.

"I did the first day. I felt like a complete idiot. On the other hand what was I supposed to do? Go into the crowd saying, 'I'm not really a witch, I'm a healer or a midwife'? I mean, that's so boring.

"I didn't know *what* to do. Then Paul, of all people, got this idea. He came up to me on the second day of the fair with that hangdog look as if I was gonna kick him or something. 'I have an idea about your character,' he explained, sort of like an apology for talking to me.

"'What is it?' His attitude got me so irritated I *did* feel like kicking him.

"'How about if when we're walking around I suddenly get taken ill. I'll roll around on the ground and complain and moan and groan. Then you can rescue me with some herbal remedies you carry around in your pouch there.'

"I totally broke up laughing. He rolls around and I spoon-feed him some powder and he says he feels better. People would think we were crazy! But then I started to feel even more guilty. I mean here Paul was ready to help me, and I couldn't help myself."

"Didn't want to upset Dan, did you?" Corey broke in.

"No, I didn't!" I snapped at her. "I mean we were really getting along."

"And he thought you were so nice!" Corey taunted. "But we know better!"

"Nice, nice, I hate that word. It's such a stupid word!" I exploded. "Have a nice day. Be nice. Nice doggy. Yuck."

"It's not a word I'd use to describe you, Alex," Sue smiled, "so don't worry so much about it."

"And just what do you mean by that?" I responded, getting really angry.

"Nothing! Didn't you just say you hated the word?"

"So what do you think I am? Mean? Nasty? What?"

Sue laughed again. "You're *you*. I mean, I admit, I've always followed Mom, and Corey follows her friends, but you just follow yourself."

"Until Dan showed up," corrected Corey.

"I tried to talk to Dan about it," I said, pretending to ignore Corey, "but he didn't want to know. Every night after work, around nine, we'd go for coffee. We talked a lot, he was easy to talk to, but not about this. He liked the play and he didn't see why we should do any more work on it. He just wanted to do it as it was, get paid, and have fun."

"Has he kissed you?" Corey asked.

"Stop asking me that!" I retorted. "It's none of your business." Of course he had, but there was no way I was telling Corey. I mean this telling thing had to have its limits. She'd just use it against me, I figured.

"So what happened to get you in trouble?" Sue persisted.

"I decided that I had to do *something*. I knew the other kids wouldn't help me, and I couldn't change the lines of the play. But I figured I could change some of *my* lines. At the end. Well, not lines, exactly. I decided I'd return as a ghost after the play appeared to be over. The ghost of the witch. And I wrote myself a monologue to say at the very end of the play."

"Did you *do* it?" Sue asked.

"She did it all right," Corey sighed.

"What happened?"

Just then the phone rang, startling everyone. I personally must've jumped two feet.

"Who'd be phoning now?" Sue gasped, leaping to her feet and grabbing for the extension on her desk. She was the only one of us who had a phone in her room because she'd paid for it with her own money. I looked at my watch. Eleven p.m.

"Hello?" Corey and I heard a murmur on the other end then saw Sue turn bright red. "Oh, hi," she said.

Sue waved at us to get out of her room. We shook our heads *no*. She tried to kick at us and just barely missed Corey, who leaped out of her way.

"It must be Mark!" Corey said in a loud voice.

"Shut up!" Sue mouthed.

"Hi, Mark!" Corey called.

"Out! Out!" Sue mouthed as she tried to make sensible noises into the receiver.

Finally I grabbed Corey and dragged her out of the room.

"Bye, Mark. Hope we meet you soon!" Corey screamed.

"Shhh," I admonished Corey, "if Mom hears us again she'll make us go to bed, and we've only finished week one."

"Yes, and you still have to tell about your little escapade," Corey grinned.

"Yeah," I agreed, rolling my eyes. We went into my room to wait.

CHAPTER 5

Corey and I sat on my bed, not talking for a while after Sue answered the phone. We could hear Sue's hushed voice, an occasional laugh or giggle.

"I wonder how serious this Mark thing is," Corey whispered. I shrugged. "Did she say anything to you?"

"No," I admitted. "But she'll have to tell. It's part of the deal."

"This isn't some sort of dictatorship, you know," Corey sneered at me, "we don't *have* to tell anything. We made the rules, we can break them."

I turned to Corey and stared at her. "Corey, what's going on? You're not yourself these days at all. What's happening?"

"Well, according to you and Sue I don't even *have* a self to be like. I'm just a big pack rat running after my friends." She paused. "It really pisses me off the way you two look down on my friends. I mean, just 'cause you've never had lots of friends like me or been as popular, you think there's something wrong with it."

"No, we don't!" I exclaimed. "It's not like that. It's not a question of being 'popular,' either. You know very well that everyone likes Sue. She's always had lots of friends."

"Sue's an egghead," Corey declared. "She has those math club friends and that inventor club thing, but they aren't really friends, they're just people who like the same things she does. Patti is her only *real* friend."

"Aren't *your* friends just people who like the same things you do?" I retorted. "I don't see the difference."

"Yeah, but they tell me everything and everyone knows everyone else's problems, we're *close*, all of us."

"All *ten* of you?" I was trying not to sound too sarcastic.

"Yeah! And the boys. There are about ten boys."

"Right, mustn't forget the boys. Fine, so if you love them all, and nothing's wrong, then why have you been in such a bad mood since that night?"

"Thanks for not telling Sue," Corey muttered.

"Don't thank me," I replied. "You'll have to tell her when it's your turn for week two."

"No, I won't, I won't tell her. She'll be all upset and I'll have to go through the whole business again. Mom still has that hurt look on her face." And Corey kicked the bed in anger.

"What happened that night?"

"Nothing!"

"Something!"

"Just leave me alone."

"Tell me. I won't tell Sue if you don't want me to."

Corey looked like she was going to shout at me but instead heaved a big sigh and sank back into the bed.

"You won't tell Sue *or* Mom?"

"I swear. But only if you tell Sue you *aren't* telling something. To be honest."

"Okay. Well, I went out with Lara, Christie, Miriam and that group, right?"

"Right."

"And John, Barry, Curtis, Les, Tod . . ."

"Tod?"

"Yeah, well, Tod is in tenth grade. He's not usually with the group but he came 'cause he's friends with Barry. And he brought his friend Jim."

"So where were you?"

"Barry's house."

"Were his parents home?"

Corey shook her head.

"So you were at a party with no parents there," I stated.

"And *you* haven't ever been to a party when no parents are home?"

"Yeah, I have. At your age. But I stopped going 'cause they were no fun."

"They *are* fun. They're more fun than *with* the parents home."

"I don't call everyone getting drunk and stupid fun."

"No, I guess you wouldn't. Pounding people to death on the basketball court is fun to *you*."

"True. Because *I'm* in control there. Those parties are a bunch of people out of control."

Corey looked at her toes.

"What happened?" I added quietly.

"This guy Tod seemed to like me. I thought he was pretty cool. Tenth grade and everything. We were drinking beer and he offered me some grass so I took a few drags."

I kept quiet and just nodded my head, knowing that if I said anything Corey might stop talking. But I was really shocked and upset. After all, she's only thirteen! Also, if I'd known then what would happen because of what she was getting into I would've done something, anything, to stop her. But I didn't know. How could I?

"Anyway, I guess what with the combination of both I got pretty high. I kept drinking, and Tod started making out with me." She paused. "Actually, I don't remember much, just that I was pretty stoned and I *really* liked what was happening. Everyone was stoned and people were making out and stuff. That's when Mom phoned. Where did she get the number, anyway? Do you know?"

"From John's mom. It was midnight, you weren't home, you hadn't called. So Mom phoned around and John's mom knew he was at Barry's and gave her Barry's number. I'd just gotten home from Martha's. But Barry told Mom you weren't there."

"I was."

"Why did he say that?"

"I told him to."

"*You* told him to?"

"I didn't want her to know I was there, okay? She would've just made me go home. And I was in no shape to go home. She would've seen I was stoned."

"We were frantic. That's when we called the police." I stared at Corey. "All these nights since school's been out have you been at these parties?"

"Yeah."

"But Mom's had the phone numbers. She's called you there. She didn't seem suspicious."

"I've gotten really good at sounding straight even when I'm not. And like, I'm not stoned every night, Alex. Mostly I just have a beer or two."

"But basically you're drinking every night."

"Yeah."

I was really upset by this time. Corey was in *way* over her head, I knew that. I also knew a lecture would accomplish nothing, so I didn't even try.

"What happened with Tod?" I asked.

Suddenly Sue stood at the door. "Are you two telling without me?"

"Well," I said quickly, "we can't just sit here staring at the floor while you talk to Mr. Wonderful. Of course we're talking."

"But were you *telling*?"

Corey shot a glance at me.

"Maybe," I answered, "but that's for Corey to say."

Corey leaped off the bed. "I want to hear all about Mark,"

she grinned. "Everything! Week two, and *you* start! *And* the phone call just now," she added.

"No. Alex was right in the middle of telling about what happened at the fair. She has to finish first. *Then* I'll tell." Sue looked hard at Corey. "Then *you*, Corey."

Sue got on the bed with us. I really wanted to hear the end of Corey's story, but I knew it was up to her and she obviously didn't want to tell Sue just yet. So I continued where I'd left off before the phone call interrupted us.

"Picture it," I grinned. "The play is over, everyone is clapping. I'm standing behind the set, which is just a simple backdrop, my heart pounding, my hands sweating. The cast starts to run onstage to take a bow. I stop them.

"'Wait,' I say, 'I've got a surprise for you!' And before any of them can stop me or do anything I leap onstage and begin my monologue. The crowd seems a bit confused but they quiet down and listen. That morning, there were about twenty. It was a small crowd, which is maybe why I worked up the nerve to do it. By the afternoon there were often fifty to a hundred people at each show. Anyway, here's my monologue."

I stood up and acted it out for them.

CHAPTER 6

"'I am but a poor ghost, caught between earth and heaven. I cannot leave my earthly bounds until I tell you, my listeners, my story. You think I am a wicked witch. But the poor women burned in the days called by you the Renaissance, a flowering of learning as you all think, were the victims of nothing but hatred, greed, and hypocrisy. Many were poor women who had no one to protect them. Many were healers whom the male doctors wanted to be rid of. Many were midwives who were good at what they did. But the Church worked the population up into a frenzy, had them looking everywhere for witches when there were none. Perhaps a few women really did believe they could do magic and considered themselves witches. But most were just plain women like me, trying to beg a meal, or help a neighbour. Why did I threaten people? I thought to frighten them into letting me go free. And I did not want to be tortured—most of those innocent women were tortured until they confessed!'

"'Hey,' some guy shouted from the crowd, 'is this a play or a lecture?'

"A few people laughed. Others told him to be quiet. I almost quit when that happened, but I wasn't finished so I kept on.

"'How many women died? Some say two hundred thousand in Europe, others say as many as *nine million*. So do not think badly of me. I'm not really a witch. Only a woman!'

"There was quite a lot of applause for twenty people, and a couple of boos. I backed up, and when I got backstage I almost got murdered.

"'Are you crazy?' Chelsea screamed in my face. 'Do you want to get us all fired? That was awful. I'm going to report you if you do that again. You can't just change everything to suit yourself. You *totally* ruined the entire play!' She was *really* upset.

"'But I think they liked it. They clapped as if they did,' I said. I looked at Dan, wondering if he'd stick up for me, but he just looked away. Lee-Ann piped up of course.

"'You had *no* business doing that on your own. And besides, it was really *boring*!'

"'I don't think it was boring,' Paul said. 'It could have been more dramatic, of course. It was a little dry but with some work it could be used.'

"It was nice of Paul to say, really. But as usual his taking my side didn't help me at all.

"'Over my dead body,' Chelsea yelled and she stomped off. 'Are you guys coming? We have a job to do!'

"They all followed her, and I trailed after them. As soon as I came out from behind the stage someone yelled at me, 'Hey you, witch!' I turned and saw a guy about my height, shaved head, spider tattoo on one arm, real charming type.

"'You talking to me?' I asked.

"The group had all stopped to see what was happening.

"'Yeah, I'm talking to you. That was a really stupid, boring speech you gave there at the end of the play.'

"'Oh,' I said, 'thank you. And who are you? The critic from *The New York Times* perhaps?'

"'Hey, baby,' he said, 'what's your problem?'

"'I don't have a problem, sir,' I said, 'and I'm not your baby.'

"'No, you're one of those femiNazis aren't you?'

"'What?'

"'You heard me. FemiNazi. I know your type.'

"Well, I just got so angry. I don't think I've ever gotten so angry. My blood was boiling. I felt like I was going to explode. How dare he call me that, that, horrible ugly name?" I paused to catch my breath feeling furious all over again, feeling the attack.

"And, and," Sue urged. "What happened?"

"I decked him," I said.

"You did what!"

"I decked him! With a good right uppercut."

"No!"

"Yes."

"Then what?"

"He fell over."

"*And?*"

"And I went over to my little group who were all gaping and I said, 'If any of you runs to Gordon with what just happened I'll do the same to you!' And I walked away, into the crowd."

"Wow!" said Sue.

"Someone *did* report me," I continued. "But I don't know who it was. None of them admitted it after."

"Could have been one of the visitors to the fair," Sue said. "All they had to do was describe your costume. Or it could've been the guy you hit!"

"Don't think so," I replied. "He'd be too embarrassed to admit a girl decked him. Anyway, Gordon called me to this little meeting and demanded to know what happened. I had to tell him about the monologue and everything. He was *not* pleased.

"'You know, Alex,' he said, 'hundreds of kids apply for these jobs. You were *very* lucky to get it.'

"'I know.'

"'If you were unhappy with your part why didn't you just come to me? I would have switched you with someone. Given you something to play you'd be comfortable with. I would've even switched your group.'

"'The thing is, Gordon,' I said, 'I didn't realize till I'd done this research that I wasn't comfortable with the part. And I kept thinking I'd get used to it but I felt funny. Because it's not true, you know, any of it.'

"I tried to tell him about what I'd learned in my research. He nodded and listened, he was really very nice about the whole thing, but then he said, 'Alex, you're obviously very bright.' I hate it when adults say that 'cause you know there's always going to be a *but* after it. 'But, this Renaissance Fair is here for one purpose and one purpose only. To entertain. Let's face it, a lot of the exhibits are really medieval, if you want to be accurate. In fact, we could take exception to just about everything here if we wanted to. But this isn't a university credit. This is fun. This is tourist dollars. This is summer jobs for kids and a great market for all our crafts-people. No one cares what happened to these women three or four hundred years ago. And if tourists start hearing that the actors are taking swings at them it would be a real scandal. In fact, we can only hope the papers don't get hold of this. And, of course, you could *ruin* this pilot project for the other kids your age.'

"He stopped and looked at me and I figured he'd fire me, for sure. 'I should probably fire you right here and now,' he sighed. 'But I can see where you're coming from. I was young once and idealistic too. You've heard of the sixties?'

"I nodded.

"'I grew up in them. Not easy to forget how idealistic we were then.' He sighed again. 'I'm going to give you another chance.'

"I almost kissed him but all I could say was 'Thank you.' I must've said it ten times.

"'Just try to have fun, Alex,' he said as I left. 'It's an acting job, nothing else. Just try to enjoy yourself.'

"I was so thankful. I kind of drifted through the fair, hardly even seeing where I was going. Suddenly Paul was there. He fell in walking beside me.

"'How'd it go?' he asked.

"'He didn't fire me,' I answered.

"'You were awesome,' he said."

"Awesome?" Sue interrupted. "He used that word?"

I glared at her. "Oh, sorry," Sue apologized, "no interruptions, sorry."

"I looked at Paul to see if he was joking but he wasn't.

"'That skinhead was despicable, he continued. 'He was a bully, and he's probably used to calling everyone names, and he probably has a girlfriend he beats up. He's terrified of feminists, he thinks they're going to break his balls.'

"I looked at Paul. I couldn't believe he'd just said that.

"'Anyway, I guess you were his worst nightmare come true,' Paul continued. Then he laughed. And I was surprised to hear what a great laugh he has—and then I realized that I'd never heard him laugh before.

"It made me laugh too. Then I stared at him. He suddenly looked so different. When he laughed he didn't look like someone was gonna kick him.

"'Something like that happened to me once,' he said, 'but I didn't handle it as well.'

"'Handle it *as well*?' I said, and I was grinning, 'cause he'd really cheered me up. 'I made a complete fool of myself onstage, lost my temper, used my fists instead of my brain, and almost got fired! *Handle it as well?*' I repeated. 'You'd have to be double the idiot I am to handle it as well!' He started to say something, I think to tell me what had happened to him, when I caught sight of Dan. 'See you later,' I called to Paul, and raced over to Dan. Paul got that hangdog look on his face and I felt a little bad just leaving him there, but I had to get over to Dan.

"'Hey, Dan,' I yelled, 'wait up.'

"Dan seemed to be pretending that I didn't exist or something. Finally he slowed down enough for me to catch up with him. When I did catch him he didn't say anything, which really surprised me and threw me so that I didn't know what to say either. So we just walked in silence for a while. Finally I got mad. I mean we'd been going out! You'd think he'd at least have asked me what happened in the meeting.

"'I didn't get fired,' I blurted out, 'in *case* you're interested.'

"He kind of gave me a funny look and he seemed surprised.

"'Really? Thought for sure they'd cut you loose.'

"'Well, they didn't. Gordon is a really great guy.'

"'Yeah. But a little lenient on his staff. That fellow could sue the fair, you know.'

"I almost laughed. I *did*, sort of, but I could see he was serious.

"'That guy is not going to sue anyone,' I snorted. 'He probably doesn't even know what the word means.'

"'Oh, you'd be surprised,' Dan said. 'Maybe you should quit.' And then he added, 'You could be ruining it for the rest of us.'

"Of course, I did feel really worried about that, but I couldn't believe he'd want me to quit. For one thing we wouldn't be together during the day. I started to wonder just how much he really liked me.

"'Are you serious?' I said.

"'Why? Are you going to hit me if I say something you don't like?'

"'You're joking, right?' I wanted to believe he was joking.

"'Am I?'

"I didn't know what to say. I was so burnt. It was, I don't know, like he really was upset that I'd hit that guy. But not 'cause he was sorry for the guy. For all kinds of other reasons."

"You weren't being nice any more," Sue said.

I stared at her.

"You're right. I wasn't being nice." I sighed.

Sue asked, "Is there more?"

I nodded. "I guess. But I think it's your turn now. Before I spill any more beans I want *you* to talk."

"Fair enough," Sue agreed.

CHAPTER 7

Before Sue began she went and got a poem she'd written, just that afternoon.

> *I went over to Reality's house*
> *the other day,*
> *but she wasn't home.*
> *So, I left a note:*
> *Dear Reality*
> *I really need to see you,*
> *please call me soon.*
> *Thanks.*
> *She never did.*

What's that expression—"Still waters run deep"? That's Sue.

"I like it," I told her.

"Weird," Corey said, and she shook her head, bewildered.

Sue snatched the poem from Corey and began.

"I met Mark one night when his family came to dinner," she said, "at Patti's dad's house. Mark's dad and Patti's dad are partners in a computer business. Mark has a brother my age, Joe, who's going into grade twelve as well, so the dads thought the four of us could get to know each other. But Joe has a girlfriend and he's not my type anyway, whereas Mark is everyone's type. Including Patti's."

"*She* likes him too?" I asked. "Uh-oh."

"Uh-oh is right," Sue nodded. "He's really smart, very cute, with curly blond hair and blue eyes . . ."

"You two must be a Nordic vision," I interjected.

Sue grinned. "We do look a lot like brother and sister. So the three of us started to hang out together all the time. Went to movies, coffee shops, he came over to swim most days, usually with a friend or two. It was great. He's going into science—environmental science."

"Oh," Corey sighed, "soul mates. So did you sit and do equations together?"

Sue gave Corey a quick glare, then continued.

"Trouble is, he's coming here now, and Patti thinks he's coming to see her, but I know he's coming to see me."

"How do you know?" I asked.

"He told me. On the phone. He doesn't want to hurt Patti's feelings, and he's been invited to stay at her house. We've nowhere to put him here, anyway."

"He can sleep on the couch," Corey suggested.

"I think he's used to better than that. At Patti's he can have his own room. And, well . . ."

"What?" I said.

"I don't know how he'd react to Mom."

At that all three of us stared glumly ahead, not really wanting to address this issue. I knew exactly what she meant, and so did Corey.

"I feel awful," Sue said into the silence, "and I don't know what to do."

"He'll just have to get used to her," I stated. "Everyone does—eventually."

"Probably the first thing she'll say to him ," Sue sighed, "is 'What is your stand on the various issues affecting women today?'"

"She did that to Peter," Corey giggled. "Remember? He backed out of the house and never returned."

"He was an idiot," I commented. "I'm sure Mark can handle himself."

"Patti's mom is nice," Sue said.

"There it is again," I exclaimed. "The dreaded *nice* word. So Mom's not 'nice.' So what? I'm proud of her."

"So am I!" Sue said. "Why do you think I help her out at the clinic all the time? I think the work she does is great." Sue paused. "But then there are her dirty jokes."

"They're funny," I said.

"True," Sue agreed. "But pretty dirty."

"My friends love them," Corey exclaimed. "They come here just for her jokes."

"Doesn't he have a sense of humour?" I asked.

"Course he does," Sue said. "But you know, we discussed a lot of science stuff, and music of course, 'cause of his band, so there wasn't a lot of time for jokes."

"So he's like, totally serious," I said, "and not political since he's into all this science stuff, and you think Mom will chase him away." I paused and I thought for a minute then said, "There's only one solution."

Sue looked hopeful.

"You can't let him stay at Patti's no matter how scared you are of his meeting Mom. He could end up *with* Patti that way. You'll just have to warn him about Mom, tell him we all think she's great but she can come on a little strong, and I'm sure it'll be fine."

Sue nodded, but didn't reply.

"Is there more?" I said, because Sue still looked really downcast.

Sue nodded again, obviously unwilling to say what it was.

"You have to tell," Corey exclaimed, "or I won't for sure!"

"I don't want to tell you. You'll hate me."

"Tell!" Corey and I said together. Sue sighed.

"I kinda gave him the impression we lived in this big two-story house. . . ."

"We do," Corey said.

"And he kinda assumed Mom was a gynecologist, not a nurse and midwife and . . ."

Sue's voice trailed off. Corey and I stared at her in disbelief. I couldn't believe what I'd just heard!

"This couldn't be Sue talking," I said finally to Corey. "Maybe she was taken over by the spirit of Patti's stepmother or some other weird ghost while she was away."

"We need an exorcist!" Corey exclaimed, jumping up making the sign of the cross.

"I'm scared!" I said.

"Oh, shut up, you two," Sue exploded, throwing a pillow at each of us. "I'm not proud of myself."

"But *why?*" I said. "I just don't get it. You love Mom's work, you're always boasting about it, you go *with* her half the time. . . . Why?"

"I don't know how it happened," Sue moaned. "We were discussing what our parents do and he has this normal household, father a big rich businessman, mom a teacher, and we have a mom who's a little unusual and a dad who disappeared ten years ago and has never been heard from since. I just wanted to seem a bit more like him so when he asked what Mom did I said 'Delivers babies,' and he just assumed that meant doctor and I didn't have the nerve to correct him. Later when I realized how stupid I'd been I couldn't correct myself because I realized how truly stupid I would look."

"What a mess," Corey declared, looking pleased.

"You don't have to be so happy about it," Sue retorted.

"I just can't believe you messed up like that," Corey gloated. "It's so great. It's always me that does the messing up, *never* you." She rubbed her hands together. "This is wonderful."

"I'm delighted it's made you so happy," Sue sighed.

"It has," Corey grinned. "It has!"

"Anyway, he wants to come up in the next couple days and I'm sure he wouldn't have cared about any of this but when he finds out that I lied to him he *will* care, and he'll hate me. So I told him that I wasn't sure now was such a good time to visit, and that maybe I could get up to Toronto again, instead."

"You've got to face it," I said. "If you tell him he can't come he'll be hurt or wonder why. Just invite him and come clean. Let him come down tomorrow." I looked at my watch. "Well, almost today. How'll he get here?"

"Drive."

"In his Porsche?" Corey said.

"No, in his 1984 Chev he bought with his own money," Sue replied. "Anyway, I don't know what to do, so let's stop talking about it for now. Time to hear more about our friend *Dan*, I think," Sue said, giving me a meaningful look. "Sounds to me like you'd become pretty involved with him."

"He's her first boyfriend, he's her first boyfriend!" Corey chanted.

"He isn't," I objected. "I've dated before."

"You've dated!" Corey grinned. "Exactly. No one dates! Who dates any more? You decide you like a guy and you start to go out with him. You're so backward."

"I never found anyone I wanted to go out with," I said, defending myself. "And I wouldn't go out with a guy just so I could have a boyfriend—like *some* people I know."

Corey glared at me but didn't reply. Sue jumped in.

"You have to at least tell us about your dates. What did you do when you went out at night?"

"The weather was good so we usually took our bikes and rode through the park, went for ice cream, that sort of thing. Or his mother would pick us up from work and drop us at a movie, then pick us up again. She drives him everywhere. I don't think he knows what the word 'bus' means. One night we went to his house for dinner."

"And?" Sue encouraged.

"They're very nice," I said.

"Oh, that word again!" Sue exclaimed.

"But that's just what they are," I said. "He has a younger sister, his mom works for his dad as a receptionist, his dad's an ear-nose-and-throat specialist."

"This is *not* getting to the heart of the matter," Sue commented. "Since you are obviously fudging I will choose a night and you have to tell all."

"I am telling!" I protested.

"Then you won't mind doing it the way I just suggested," Sue said smugly.

"Which night?" I grimaced.

"The night you went there for dinner."

"I told you, we went there for dinner."

"What did you eat?" Corey asked.

"I don't know. . . . Oh, yeah, meat balls and potatoes and salad. Swedish meat balls."

"And *after* dinner?" Sue quizzed.

"We went downstairs to watch a movie."

"All of you?" Sue pressed.

"Just Dan and me."

"And?"

"Nothing! We watched *Sleepless in Seattle*. It was very romantic."

"How far are you going?" Sue asked.

Did she really think I'd tell her? Well, maybe I would, later, without Corey there. Corey doesn't have to know *everything*. Besides we'd basically only done some heavy kissing and above-the-waist stuff.

"Never mind," I shrugged.

"Come on, Alex."

"Not far."

"You swear?"

"Yeah, I swear, but I can tell you I'm tempted. And it's not like it's him wanting to do more than me. He's so hot."

"He may be hot, but are you sure he actually likes you?" Sue asked.

"No," I sighed. "It's incredibly stupid. We hardly have anything in common, I'm beginning to think—but I'm crazy about him. And he can't figure me out at all."

"You aren't enough like his mom," Sue grinned.

"Don't use that nice word," I threatened. "Actually things were going really well until I almost got fired. We had planned to go out that night and we met at the park on our bikes. Then it seemed like he didn't even want to be there. So I said that to him."

"What did you say?" Corey asked.

"'You look like you'd rather be anywhere else!'

"'No,' he protested, 'I want to go out tonight.'

"But then he said something that really shocked me. 'I'm sorry I didn't stick up for you today,' he kinda muttered.

"'With Gordon, you mean?' I said. 'That's okay. There wasn't anything you could've said to him, really. Unless you'd like to do a different play. Help me convince the others, maybe.'

"'Alex!' he said and he seemed really exasperated. 'We can't do another play. When are we going to rehearse it? It took us a whole week to do this one!'

"I was confused. 'What do you mean by "stick up for me" then?'

"'I mean with that skinhead. I should have taken him out for you.'

"'It seems to me,' I said, 'that I took him out just fine.'

"'Well, I know you did, but *I* should have.'

"'Why, because you're the man?' I said, trying not to laugh.

"'Yeah,' he admitted. 'I know it's old-fashioned, but I still feel bad.'

"'It's not just old-fashioned,' I lectured him. 'It's stupid. I obviously didn't need you.'

"'No,' he said and he looked really mad at me. 'You *obviously* didn't.'

"'Well, I'm sorry,' I said.

"I mean, there *I* was apologizing to *him* because I didn't need him to defend me and then he felt bad for not doing it!"

Sue laughed. "Men!" she said.

"I think it's sweet," Corey stated.

"But he *didn't* help me when I needed it," I replied, "then made me feel bad about it afterwards."

"Men," Sue repeated.

"'Why *didn't* you defend me?' I asked him.

"'Well,' he said, 'for one thing I was mad at you for doing that piece on your own.'

"'And why were you mad about that? I mean, why couldn't you back me on it?'

"We were just standing like idiots at that point, near the swings, holding our bikes.

"'Let's ride,' he suggested, so we got on our bikes and started to ride through the park on the trail closest to the river.

"I was glad we were finally talking about everything, although I was scared that once we talked we'd have to stop seeing each other, because I'd find out he really didn't like me."

"If he didn't like you why would he go out with you?" Corey interrupted.

"She's 'telling' now," Sue said. "Quiet."

"You know what I mean," I said. "He likes who he *thinks* I am, my looks, the idea of me, but deep down he doesn't like *me*. He never really seemed to approve of anything I'd do. So I kind of held my breath and waited to hear what he'd say.

"'The thing is,' he said, not looking at me but keeping his

eye on the bike trail, 'that I didn't support you because you weren't right.'

"'And you know everything, I suppose,' I barked at him, feeling really angry.

"'No, of course not, but I know that when you're doing a group thing you don't just go off on your own and do your own thing. No wonder everyone was mad at you.'

"'Chelsea,' I snorted. 'And Lee-Ann. All they care about is having fun.'

"'That's not quite fair,' he objected. 'They do care about that mostly, but they are really good at their jobs and they're hard-working. Have you ever seen them goof off?'

"I had to admit he was right.

"'Well,' I said, 'you should have supported me earlier. When I wanted to change the whole play. Paul did.'

"'You didn't seem to care,' he argued. 'When I said I thought we should leave it alone, you just dropped the whole idea. *That* was the time to fight for it. If you'd tried to convince me then, maybe I would've taken your side.'

"'You didn't want me to make trouble,' I grumbled.

"'That's true,' he admitted. 'What's so bad about taking the easier route? You were suggesting a far more difficult piece. But in the end you *chose* to go along with it.'

"That *really* made me mad, because deep down I knew he was right. I'm so used to doing things on my own, my own way, it never occurred to me that I could try different ways to get people on my side. My way was to fight everyone and then win or lose."

"Did you hear something?" Corey interrupted again.

"Don't interrupt," Sue said.

"I heard something," Corey insisted. She got up and went to the window. "Someone's out there!"

"Who?" both of them said, as they ran to look.

"He's throwing pebbles up," Corey laughed. "Right out of the movies."

I opened the window and peered out.

"It's Paul!" I said, really surprised. "What on earth is *he* doing here?"

"Well, he can't be here now. We're telling!" Sue said.

"It must be important," I said, starting out the door. "I haven't gotten to the part where Paul and I become good friends," I called to Sue. "But we are. I'll go talk to him in the kitchen and come right back, I promise." I glared at them. "And no telling till I'm back."

"Hurry up!" Sue said as I rushed down the hall to the front door.

CHAPTER 8

I was really surprised to see Paul. We had become good friends by then, but still, he'd never just turned up at the house like that, uninvited. And so late. I figured something pretty bad had happened.

I opened the door and stared at him. "You look terrible. Come on in."

"Thanks," Paul mumbled as he followed me into the kitchen. "Sorry to do this to you. Will your mom be mad?"

"Who knows?" I shrugged. "When I expect her to get mad she doesn't, and when I don't expect her to get mad she does. She probably *won't* get mad 'cause if you're here this late there must be a good reason for it. She's like that."

"Must be nice," Paul said and then sat down at the kitchen table and burst out crying.

I was paralysed. I'd never seen a boy my age cry. I had no

idea what to do. Awkwardly I moved over to him and patted his shoulder.

"What is it? What's the matter?" I asked.

Paul swiped at the tears and tried to catch his breath. "I'm sorry. This is so stupid. I came over here all excited, really up, had to tell you in person and now look." He gulped. "Could I have some water?"

"Sure," I said, delighted to be able to do something. I ran to the fridge, took out the water filter jug and poured him a glass of ice-cold water.

Paul gulped it down. He looked up at me and said swiftly, "I'm coming out."

For a moment I had no idea what he meant. You *are* out, I thought. You're here. And then, in a flash, it dawned on me.

"What an idiot I am!" I exclaimed. "I should have realized when there was that thing with the skinhead and you said you'd had a similar experience. What, did someone call you a fag or a queer or something?"

Paul nodded, but didn't speak. He looked like he was waiting for me to say something else.

"Oh," I declared, "like, it's fine with me. Not that you need *my* approval. But we were brought up in this house to respect everyone, or *else*!"

Paul seemed to relax then. "That's good," he sighed.

I sat down beside him at the table.

This was a big deal.

"How did you find out?" I said. "Are you *sure*?"

"I'm sure," he replied. "I've known since I was around ten

years old. All the boys were talking about girls and I wasn't the least bit interested. I was interested in *them* while they talked about the girls."

"Why now?" I asked.

"It's this play," he said. "It's bothered me all along, ever since I started to do the research. Did you know that just when they were taking all the power away from women they did the same to homosexuals? Being gay was no crime—right up to the fourteenth century. In fact, it was accepted pretty much everywhere. Then the Church decided it was wrong and began to persecute homosexuals along with other heretics, like Jews. Witches were a small part of that in the 1200s and 1300s. It wasn't until the 1500s and 1600s they *really* went after women in a big way. Know where the term *faggot* comes from?"

I shook my head.

"It means a bundle of sticks, right? Well, they used homosexual men as kindling to start the fires that burned the witches. Hence the term *fag*."

"That's disgusting," I said.

"Anyway, I did all this research and I agreed with you about the witch thing but I was afraid to say it. But it's been eating away at me. Every day I go to work, we do our play, and I feel bad—like we're spreading a lie, telling things all wrong."

"That's the way I feel," I agreed.

"So I was thinking that we could go to Gordon if we had another play, and ask him if we could do it as well. See, we'd still do the first one, so as not to upset the others. But maybe you and I could do something different during the day, just once or twice."

"I love it," I exclaimed. "It's a great idea! Are you gonna tell the other kids about being gay?"

"Eventually," Paul said. "That's why I wanted to tell you first. Moral support."

"Listen, Paul, I'll support you one hundred percent, but I think you should think twice before you announce this to the world. The kids at school are gonna be really hard on you. Maybe you should wait till you're a little older and you can handle it better."

Paul looked at me thoughtfully.

"You may be right," he sighed. "I want to be free and open so badly but—maybe not yet. Still, at least if we could do this piece and *you* know, well, I'll feel better. Want to start now? We could jot down some notes, maybe make an outline?"

I shook my head. "I can't, Paul. I know this is a tough night for you, but Sue just got back and we have this pact between us that if someone's been away, or we haven't had a chance to talk in a few weeks, we get together at night and have a 'Telling' session. They're waiting upstairs for me now."

"Oh, I'm sorry!" Paul said. "I didn't mean to interrupt."

"Stop being sorry about everything!" I exclaimed. "It's so irritating."

"I know it is, I'm really sorry," Paul replied.

I raised my eyebrows in response and we both laughed.

I grabbed Paul's hand. "Come on upstairs and meet them,"

I said. "You've never actually met Corey either, have you?" I asked, as I pulled him along.

"No, I saw her with you at the fair one day," he whispered, as I put a finger over my mouth and pointed to Mom's room.

"Yeah," I said, "that's right. Well, Sue'll want to meet you too. Then you'll have to go and we can work on this tomorrow at lunch. Okay?"

"Sure," Paul agreed.

"Hey, guys," I said as we reached my bedroom, "this is Paul."

"Hi!" said Sue.

"Hi," grinned Corey.

Paul and I stood awkwardly in the door for a moment. Corey pulled down her Mickey Mouse nightshirt. Then Sue spoke.

"Having fun at the fair, Paul?"

"Well," he answered, "it's been an experience."

"Hmm," Sue replied, "sounds like a story there."

"Alex can tell you," Paul said. "I better go. Sorry for breaking up your talk."

"Stop that!" I said, smacking him lightly on the arm.

"Right. I'm *not* sorry," Paul grinned. "See you."

"See you," echoed the girls, and I took Paul back downstairs.

"I'm glad you came over," I said when we got to the door. "I mean, I'm glad you trusted me enough to tell me." I paused. "It'll be all right. You'll see." I hoped it would. I really hoped so. Impulsively I reached out and gave him a big hug.

He hugged me back and as we drew away from each other he said, "My parents don't know."

It looked like he might start to cry again.

"Are you going to tell them?"

Paul shrugged.

"Are they anti-gay or something?"

Paul nodded. "They're very religious. Take the Bible literally. It's an abomination."

"If you come out at the fair, and at school, they'll find out," I cautioned.

"I know," Paul said. "Maybe they'll kick me out. Great to think that your own parents basically hate everything about you."

"No," I contradicted him, "not everything. They love you, I'm sure. It's just, well, for a while they'll think this is the only thing about you that matters. But that's not all of who you are. You're still *you*."

"Thanks," Paul said. "See you on the morrow."

"The morrow, good sir," I replied with a smile and a bow. I shut the door gently behind him then stood there for a minute before going upstairs.

What was I going to tell my sisters? I mean, this was obviously a secret—in fact, I'd convinced him to keep it a secret. But everyone knows how it is with secrets—you *always* tell someone, usually your best friend. I mean, even being sworn to secrecy doesn't include your best friend, does it? And my sisters and I have a pact *never* to tell anyone anything about our tellings—even our best friends. That does make life hard sometimes.

Martha always says she's not really my best friend, my sisters are. And I guess if you judge a friend by how much you tell them, she might have a point. On the other hand, there're things I tell her (like about Dan) that I wouldn't tell Sue and Corey, in case they used it against me. And I know they try to hold stuff back from me too.

I wasn't getting too far in my deliberations. I decided to go up and see if I could get away with not telling them.

Sue just raised her eyebrows in a question when I walked back in, but Corey really went after me.

"So? So? What was *so* important he had to end up here at this hour?"

"Nothing," I said.

"Yeah, right," said Corey. "You know we're sworn to keep everything secret here so you have no good reason not to tell us. He even said, 'Alex'll tell you.' He wants us to know."

I kind of grabbed at that, because the truth was I was dying to tell them. I guess I didn't need too much persuasion.

One thing I've learned from this—how powerful words are. How they can change our lives. Maybe if I hadn't given in so quickly to Corey . . . But how was I to know what would be the result? So I told.

"This goes *no further*," I warned Corey.

Eagerly she nodded her head. Sue nodded as well, although I didn't need to worry about her.

"He's gay," I announced. "He wants to come out and I'm the first person he's told."

"Heavy," Corey said.

"Poor guy," said Sue. "I don't envy him. He's going to go through hell once everyone finds out."

"Think so?" I asked.

"I *know* so. You probably don't remember but when Norman Johnson came out the whole school was in an uproar. The jocks wouldn't leave him alone. They were always bugging him in the school cafeteria, in the hallways, they even beat him up a couple times."

"The jocks?" I said. "I would've thought the skinheads would be the worst ones."

Sue shook her head. "The jocks seem to take it as an insult to their manhood. A direct threat or something. Maybe they were afraid that somewhere inside *they* could be hiding those feelings. Well, that's Mom's theory anyway. Oh, they were vicious."

"But that was a couple years ago," I said. "Things aren't as bad now I don't think."

"Yes, they are," Corey said. "Kids in my school are always making gay jokes and stuff."

"He wants us to do a play together," I informed them. "I'm going to."

"I think you should," Sue said in approval. "But don't expect it to be easy going. Once you've hooked up with him you'll get a lot of the flak he gets, just for being friends with him."

"That's true," I sighed. "But I can't let him down."

"He chose you," Sue said. "That doesn't mean you have to choose him back."

I thought about it for a minute. "You're right," I said, "but we've really gotten to be pals and I like him. I couldn't let him down. Don't forget, he stood up for me about this witch thing all along. He's the *only* one that did."

Sue nodded. "Go for it then," she said.

"You're just looking for trouble at that fair, aren't you?" Corey added.

I shot a look at her. It made me really mad when she lectured me, as if she knew *anything*! "Speaking of trouble, you haven't finished your story. Are you going to tell Sue what happened that night?" I gave her a fake smile.

"You promised not to tell her!" Corey exclaimed.

"I'm not telling her," I retorted. "I'm asking if you're going to tell. We agreed you'd have to admit to *not* telling if you decide not to."

"I don't know why you two are having this fight," Sue interjected. "Corey was telling me about it while you were down there with Paul."

"I told you not to talk without me!" I protested.

"You two talked without me." Sue reminded me.

I plunked myself on the floor, as my two sisters were on the bed. "Where have you got to?"

"I just told her about getting home from that party with Tod and finding the police here."

"But what happened at the party with Tod?" I wanted to know. "Did you tell Sue?"

"She told me," Sue acknowledged.

I looked expectantly at Corey. After all, she *had* to tell me if she'd told Sue. Those were the rules.

"We were making out," Corey said quietly, "and we were both out of it, and it went further faster than I thought it would." She paused. "Not that I was really thinking. Suddenly I got scared and I broke away and said I wanted to go home. But Tod got mad and didn't want to leave, and I couldn't call Mom 'cause I'd already told her I wasn't there.

"I went round to everyone saying it was late and was anyone getting picked up, but they'd all told their parents they were sleeping somewhere, like at a friend's. It was then I found out that Barry's parents weren't just out, they were out of town."

"But Barry lives in the west end," I said. "That's really far. What did you do?"

"I had to get out of there," Corey said. "I knew that. I was really scared by then."

"What about all your best friends. What were they doing? Didn't they help you?"

Corey stared at her feet. "They'd left."

"They'd *left*?" I said.

"They told me the next day they'd tried to get me to leave with them when Miriam's mom came, but I was so spaced out I told them to get lost. I didn't want Tod to think I was a baby and had to leave with the other younger kids."

"So who was there?"

"By then mostly Tod and his friends."

"And what did Barry think about it all?" I asked.

Corey grimaced. "He was in the same boat as me. He didn't know how to get rid of them without looking like a baby."

"What was he doing home alone?" Sue wanted to know. "Surely his parents didn't go out of town and leave him all alone."

"No, his brother, who's seventeen, was staying with him, but he was out. When he came home he just figured they were Barry's friends and didn't bother to throw them out. Like, I guess he thought as long as they weren't wrecking the house they could stay over.

"I asked Barry what to do, but he didn't know. By then I was getting sober fast and I wanted to be home. And I started to think about Mom and how worried she'd be. So I just left."

"What time was it?" I asked.

"Not sure. Maybe one a.m."

"So you just walked out into the night at one a.m. in the west end, with no way to get home?" I persisted.

Corey nodded. "I hitch-hiked home," she said in a really quiet voice.

"You hitch-hiked?" Both Sue and I spoke at the same time.

Again Corey nodded. "But only up to Ross Street. I was lucky I got a ride from some kids from Pearson High. They teased me a lot but it was okay. Then I walked the rest of the way."

"Which got you home around one-thirty, just a few minutes after the police arrived," I said.

"Right," Corey agreed. "When did Mom call them?"

"About one o'clock," I said. "We'd called your friends, and they all said you were at Barry's. But we called Barry's and he denied that you were there, so Mom called the police. We were panicked."

"That's quite a story," Sue stated, gazing at Corey.

"I know it was stupid, okay?" Corey declared. "You don't have to give me that look."

"Corey," Sue said, "from what you've said, you're still hanging with this group and they're all into drinking and some drugs. It's not a good scene. As long as you're with them you won't be able to stop."

"I'm not giving up my friends," Corey declared fiercely. "I don't care if you don't like them. You just don't understand!"

Sue and I exchanged a brief glance, not lost on Corey, and then Sue changed the subject. After all, there was no use pushing Corey on this one. She wasn't ready to admit there was even a problem—not yet.

"So what about Dan?" Sue said to me. "Are you two still an item?"

"Yeah, I guess. I don't know. We had that talk a few days ago and we haven't been out since. We're supposed to go out tomorrow night. "What are you going to do about Mark?" I asked.

"Don't know," Sue replied. "I'll decide in the morning."

We knew that the "Telling" was over for the night. We all fought for space in the bathroom as we did our teeth and washed up. Then we returned to Sue's room for our closing ritual.

Holding hands we circled together, chanting:

> *When shall we three meet again*
> *In thunder, lightning, or in rain*
> *When the hurly-burly's done,*
> *When the battle's lost and won.*

Faster and faster we went until we each snapped away from the circle, like crack-the-whip on ice, and spun into our own rooms, our own beds, and sleep.

CHAPTER 9

Streaks of electricity
bolt through the twilight.
Losing themselves in a monstrous
orchestra of drums.
We two sit beneath the universe,
insignificant, in contrast to the
penetrating scream of the earth.
Intricate lies and cluttered
emotion swirl through the trees,
entangling branches and tossing
leaves to the sea.
Yet, I sit in silence,
hearing only the rhythmic
rise and fall
of your
breath.

I found that poem by my bed just after Mark got here. Sue's way of telling me what was going on between them, I guess.

We had our next "Telling" about a week later. By then, the three of us were barely speaking. In fact, Corey and I weren't speaking. Sue had to make us participate. I had never been so mad at Corey before—never in our entire lives. I really hated her for a little bit then and I thought I'd never feel any different.

Sue made us hold hands even though I'd just as soon have broken Corey's fingers as hold them, and we had to do our chant.

> *The weird sisters, hand in hand,*
> *Posters of the sea and land,*
> *Thus do go about, about.*

Faster and faster we moved until we collapsed to the floor. This time there was no laughter though, just a lot of tension in the air.

Sue spoke first. "I've called a 'Telling' because I leave for camp tomorrow and I don't want to go away with things the way they are."

"This is stupid," Corey muttered.

"We all know what happened," I snapped. "What's the use of going over it?"

"We know the events, or each of us knows *part* of the events but we don't know the whole story or why everyone did what they did. We have to tell that."

I guess what Sue said did make sense. She was right. We all knew part of the story—our own part—but it turned out we really didn't know the other side of it. That makes me think a lot about this whole storytelling business. And I don't mean just the way Sue and Corey and I tell our stories. I mean, like when you see a newscast, they're telling you one *version* of a story, aren't they? I bet if a Confederate or a Union soldier told about the same time in history you'd get two different versions. Or take the witch-burnings. We only know the version handed down by the men who persecuted the witches. Or take World War II. If Hitler had won the war, the story of World War II would be different, wouldn't it? No one would read in the history books about the murder of the Jews. That would've been hushed up. And now that I think about it, since *I'm* telling this story no one is *really* getting to know all about Corey, or Sue, or even me, because *I* pick and choose what I put in. What if I'm really an axe murderer? I wouldn't include that here, would I? I'm trying to be honest and tell it just like it happened. But it's not as simple as it seemed at first.

At any rate, Sue kept on trying to convince us.

"I promised Mom I'd try to get everyone to make up before I leave."

"Mommy's perfect little girl," Corey smirked.

"Something *you* never have to worry about being," I snapped at her.

"Oh, here's Ms. Wonderful again," Corey sneered. "Well,

for your information, I was trying to *help* you! And look where it got me!"

I leaped up. "You were trying to *help!* That's the most ridiculous thing I've ever heard. Next time do me a favour and go help someone else!"

"Quiet! Both of you!" Sue ordered. "We're going to have this 'Telling' and that's that. Alex, you start."

"And what about you?" I said to Sue. "Seems to me there are a few little things you have to share about your precious Marky."

"Fine," Sue agreed, giving me an unhappy glare. "I'll share too. Happy?"

"Ecstatic," I declared. "Am I supposed to start? It's simple, really. *My* story is simple and straightforward."

"Are you going to start or not?" Corey grumbled.

"Yes! The morning after Paul came over we met at the fair, as usual. We had lunch together.

"'Listen,' I said, over some pizza, 'maybe we should forget writing a new play. Gordon won't let us do it, the others don't care, and I don't want to get into any more trouble.'

"'Do you want to set the record straight or not?' he answered.

"'Not,' I replied.

"'So it's okay for everyone who comes to the fair to go away with the idea of witches being evil beings who really practised black magic?'

"'No one believes in magic any more,' I countered.

"'That's true,' he replied. "So they assume these were evil

women, practising a bunch of nonsense, who were rightly punished because they had hearts as black as coal. And over the centuries, any time women have attained any power or respect someone called them a witch and they were finished. It went on for hundreds of years like that.'

"'It's better now,' I replied, my heart not in my protest.

"'Of course it is,' Paul answered. 'Why, just the other day the Pope warned that radical feminism was causing Roman Catholics to perform pagan rituals and practise nature worship.'

"'Did he?' I said.

"'Yes. And you know what one of the leaders of the Moral Majority, in the U.S., said?'

"'I dread to think,' I replied.

"'He said that the feminist movement encourages women to leave their husbands, kill their children, practise witchcraft, destroy capitalism and become lesbians.'

"'Wow', I sighed. 'That's heavy.'

"'So is it *just* history we're talking about, or does history mean something to us today?'

"'But I'm not a feminist,' I protested.

"'Why not?' Paul asked, looking surprised.

"'I hate those labels,' I grumbled. 'I don't want to be part of some group. I just want to be myself.'

"'And working alone, by yourself, you can get a lot accomplished, can't you? Just like you did the other day with your monologue.' He was very sarcastic and I was starting to get angry.

"'Never mind,' I snapped. 'I *could've* done it alone if I'd done it better.'

"'You can't do theatre alone. Or anything, really,' Paul stated.

"'Can too,' I declared. 'What about a one-woman show?'

"'I suppose you don't need a director, a designer, a lighting designer, a technical crew—'

"'Okay, okay,' I interrupted. 'I get the picture. But no one can tell me I have to be a feminist.'

"'That's true,' Paul grinned. 'No one can tell you anything. But what's wrong with being in a group that supports you?' Paul paused. 'Men have it easier than women. We get more power as we get older. We don't need male groups, we're just one big group!'

"'I know you're right,' I said, and sighed. 'After all, I'm the one who's been arguing to change the play all this time. I just don't want any more trouble.'"

I looked at my sisters. "I mean, Dan and I had just had this great talk, and I knew that if I did this thing with Paul it'd be trouble." I glared at Corey. "Of course I didn't realize *where* the trouble would come from." Corey glared back.

"Anyway, we started to write this piece about a young woman and young man who were accused of heresy and witchcraft. We decided that we couldn't do it with two characters, so we wrote it for five in the hopes of convincing the others once it was done. And since we weren't sure that the girls *would* agree we hoped that some kids from another group might do it if they refused. We spent that day after work on it, as you know—since we were here writing till two a.m.—and then we spent the next day at lunch working on it. By then we had something."

"I missed it," Sue said.

"I know *that*," I barked.

"Can I read it now?"

"Well, that's pretty boring," Corey objected. "What am I supposed to do while you sit there and read it?"

"Fine," Sue said. "We'll read it aloud like last time."

"Don't feel like it," Corey muttered.

"You can't say you really know what's in it, though, can you?" Sue said. Corey was silent. "No. You wouldn't have absorbed much the day you saw it."

"She absorbed a lot!" I jumped in.

"You know what I mean," Sue continued.

"So let's read it, like we did the last one. Go get it, Alex."

I got up reluctantly and went to my room to fetch the manuscript. When I returned Sue and Corey were sitting, silent. They obviously had nothing to say to each other. Or perhaps too much to say.

"I'll do my part, the Woman," I said. "Sue, you can be the Inquisitor and the Doctor, and Corey can be the Man."

They nodded in agreement, picked up their scripts and began to read.

Germany

(Man *enters; looks around.* Woman *enters*)

MAN: Fraülein Gerber, please come. My sister has been taken ill.

WOMAN: Is she not almost ready to give birth? Perhaps it is only the normal feeling of sickness just before the baby comes.

MAN: No. Her fever is high, she is delirious. Please come.

WOMAN: Of course.

(Both exit, and then re-enter. They sit)

WOMAN: I'm sorry I could not save her.

MAN: What happened?

WOMAN: It was some kind of illness that attacked her lungs. Still, I believe the baby will live. She seems strong.

(Enter Doctor *and* Inquisitor *and* Guard)

DOCTOR: There she is.

INQUISITOR: You practise witchcraft, disguised as medicine. You must be stopped.

MAN: No! She has done nothing. She just saved my sister's baby.

DOCTOR: You mean to say she just killed your sister. I have told you people over and over to come to me if there is a problem. I am a medical doctor. I have been trained in Cologne. This woman is a

	danger to you and your relatives.
MAN:	No, that isn't true.
INQUISITOR:	And who are you?
MAN:	My name is Hugo Bergmann, my lord.
INQUISITOR:	A fine-looking young man. You will come with me, Hugo. (*Turns to* Guard) And bring the woman.
WOMAN:	But why?
MAN:	Come with you? Why?
INQUISITOR:	Bring them!

*(Guard pushes the two ahead of him. Exit all.
Enter* Woman, *sits.* Man *enters a moment later, is
thrown to the ground by the* Guard. *He is crying.*
Woman *goes over to comfort him)*

WOMAN:	Master Bergmann, what is it?
MAN:	I cannot say. The Inquisitor, he has forced me to—oh, I cannot say.
WOMAN:	You need say nothing more. I have heard much of their sexual appetites.

When we got to that last line I suddenly stopped reading. "I'd say it was around here when we were so rudely interrupted. What do you think, Corey? Am I right?"

"How should I know?" Corey responded, her look sullen.

"How should you know? Oh, right. You can't *remember* can you?"

"Not really!"

"It's good so far," Sue interrupted. "How did you get everyone to do it?"

"Well," I answered, "Paul and I came up with a strategy. We figured we'd go after each person separately. I decided to start with Dan. I figured I'd tackle him at supper. Paul figured he could handle the clones and that would be everyone.

"That night at supper time I made sure Dan and I went off on our own—away from the group. Usually we eat in the same spot every night, but I convinced him to go to the other side of the fairground at Shepherd's Green to get some fish and chips.

"'Dan,' I said to him, 'you were mad at me before for just doing something, without consulting you.'

"'Yeah,' he agreed.

"'So now I'm consulting you.'

"'Uh-oh.'

"I tried to ignore his sarcasm. I needed his help.

"'Paul convinced me to take another crack at the play— rewriting it, I mean. That is, writing a different one.'

"'Paul!' Dan exclaimed. 'Look, I didn't want to say anything but ever since that day Gordon got on your case you and Paul have been a real thing. I mean, just tell me if I'm in the way.'

"I grinned. 'It's not like that, believe me.'

"'Why should I?' he said, and he was really sulking. 'You're with him all day, laughing and giggling about everything and everybody, you hardly have time to say two words to me.'

"'I'm saying more than two words now,' I teased him.

"'Thanks. Thanks a lot.'

"'No, really, I'm telling you Paul is no threat here. He and I are just good friends. There is *nothing* romantic.'

"Dan sighed and looked extremely unconvinced.

"'And now I'm including you, aren't I? We're working on this script and it's going to be good, but we *badly* need you in it. I *promise* I won't do it without Gordon's approval. And Paul is going to convince the girls to join in too.'

"'What about the extra work? Learning lines and everything?'

"'It'll be simple. And short. But effective!'

"I clasped my hands together. *'Please.'* I dropped to my knees. *'Please.'*

"'Oh, all right!'

"And that was it. And I'm sure," I added, glaring at Corey, "that he was *so* glad he agreed!"

"Shut up!" Corey yelled.

"Corey," Sue said, "it's time we heard from you. Come on. You better let us in on how all this happened."

"Why should I?"

"Because if you don't," Sue replied, "our 'Telling' is ruined. If one quits, it's all ruined. Is that what you want?"

"Fine," said Corey, her voice angry and defensive. "I'll tell."

"It'd better be good," I muttered.

"What's the point!" Corey exclaimed, getting up.

"Just tell!" ordered Sue.

Reluctantly, Corey sat down. She hugged her knees into her chest, sighed, and began to speak.

I was determined not to let anything she said convince me to forgive her. I was determined to be mad at her forever.

CHAPTER 10

"My friend Lonnie had been at camp for three weeks and had just gotten back, so of course we all went over to her house to see her. And Maureen'd just got back the day before so we all had lots to tell each other. We were there at lunch time and we were really hyper and celebrating being together again—"

"You'd been apart three weeks, not three years!" I interrupted. I really did want to murder her.

"This is stupid!" Corey exclaimed. She appealed to Sue. "What's the point? She's never going to forgive me or let me live this down. Nothing I say is gonna make any difference."

Sue turned to me. "Corey's right. If you can't listen with an open mind you shouldn't listen at all. What's the point?"

"There is no point," I said sullenly. I didn't even *want* to forgive her. And I knew if I listened, I might just soften.

"Come on, Alex, give her a chance," Sue said. "She's your

baby sister. Cut her some slack. It's not as if you've been perfect your whole life."

"I never said I have. But I've sure never done anything like this to her. I always looked out for her. Always. Who's taken care of bullies for you all these years?" I said to Corey. "Your friends or me? Who's listened to all your problems? Who's covered for you with Mom?"

"I'm sorry, I'm sorry, I'm sorry!" Corey cried. "What else can I say? I can't undo it! I wish it had never happened."

There was a pause as I stared at Corey and tried to decide whether to cut her any slack or not. Corey's eyes were filled with tears. "I'm sorry," she repeated quietly.

"Alright," I sighed finally, "I'll listen." And that was *really* hard for me to say.

Suddenly Corey seemed to want to tell.

"Like I said," she continued, "everyone was all hyper. And suddenly Lonnie pulled out this big thing of wine—you know the kind you pour out of a box, with a spout?"

Sue and I nodded, not saying anything.

"And she said she'd found it at the back of the liquor cabinet, it had probably been there for ages and her dad would never miss it. So we drank wine and ate cheese sandwiches. And then we were trying to think of what to do all afternoon and someone said, 'Let's go to the fair.' And I remembered you were going to be putting on your new play so I figured that was a great idea. 'We can see Alex's play!' I told everyone. So we got the bus, the fair bus from downtown. I didn't feel drunk, just happy. Same with the rest of the kids. Sure we were giggling and laughing a lot, but I thought you'd be really glad if I brought a whole group to watch your play."

I just kept my mouth shut. I knew if I said anything it would be negative and Corey would probably stop. By this time I was getting interested despite myself.

"I didn't know I wasn't thinking straight," Corey explained. "I thought I was thinking totally clearly." She paused. "Well, on the bus Lonnie started passing around a big 7–11 mug with a straw. I figured it was a Slurpee or something till I took my first sip. It wasn't a Slurpee. I'm still not sure what it was—some kind of hard liquor. It tasted awful, but everyone else was drinking it and laughing and playing along so I figured I would too.

"We got to the fair and by then I guess we were all pretty blasted. But I still didn't know how blasted I was. I just felt great and I was giddy, and everything seemed funny and we were all screaming and laughing. So we got to the area where you were doing your play and everyone was still loud but I made them quiet down when I saw the play was on. I did. I ran to each person and shushed them and told them you were my sister and you'd worked hard on the play."

"All of which everyone in the audience heard," I remarked.

"I thought I was whispering," Corey said. "So then we watched and it was when you got to that part, about the Inquisitor forcing the young man to have sex, that it suddenly dawned on me that this was Paul's way of telling something about being gay—I mean, how they were burned, not that the Inquisitors went after them, and I felt so proud of him, and I wanted to support him—so I shouted."

"What did you shout?" Sue asked.

"I'm not sure," Corey mumbled.

But I remembered. It's something I'll never forget. When the words came out of her mouth my stomach sank and twisted. I thought I might be sick.

"She shouted," I said to Sue, "'Right on, Paul! Gay Pride! We love you, Paul.' And something about, 'But couldn't he dress a little smarter?' At which point the rest of her group went completely nuts, shouting and screaming nonsense until there was no point in going on with the play. The security guards had to throw them all out. And it was our *first* performance," I added. "While you'd been bumming around with your friends," I said to Corey, "I was working really hard to get this together. Paul convinced Lee-Ann and Chelsea to do it, because he said it would give them extra exposure. I convinced Dan. We had to write it, which was hard work. Everyone had to memorize their lines. And then we had to convince Gordon. We did it all, I got everyone behind the project, I got everyone working together and I was able to work with the group, and then your mob showed up and totally ruined it."

"But you did it again, didn't you?" Corey asked.

"No," I replied. "Lee-Ann and Chelsea were so mad at me—they knew you were my sister—they said they'd never work on another project of mine again. So we're back to the old play and I'm the evil witch who cackles around the fair.

To say nothing of how Paul felt, being humiliated like that! Chelsea and Lee-Ann look at him as if he's some sort of monster. Dan is nervous around him all the time! Half the kids at the fair shun him completely, he's teased constantly, especially about the cute little tights he wears! It's turned his entire life upside down! Corey, I told you about Paul, here, in a 'Telling,' where everything is secret. And then you blabbed it to the entire world! I'm lucky Paul is still my friend, because if I were him I'd hate me!"

Corey sighed. "I promise I won't ever take another drink."

"You don't get it, Corey, do you?" I exploded. "It's not about whether you drink or not. It's about you and your friends. You do everything they do. What does it matter if you say you won't take another drink? That group'll think something else up and you'll do that instead."

"I'm not giving them up!" Corey exclaimed.

"Then you'd better learn how to separate from them and make your own choices," Sue advised. "Or this is just the start of your troubles."

We all sat there in silence for a few moments. I don't know what the other two were thinking, but I was thinking about Paul. He'd taken my advice, he'd decided to wait before he came out. He made the right choice but where did it get him? And I'd made what I thought was a good choice, doing another play, working in a group, like on the court but off, and that didn't work out either.

Aloud, I finally said, "Sometimes we make all the right choices and everything still turns out wrong."

"It's true," Sue said, "you can't control everything."

"You can't control *anything*," I countered.

"All you can do is make your choices but I guess it all comes down to how you handle what's being thrown at you," Sue said, looking at me.

"Are you *implying* something?" I asked.

"I'm just wondering why you gave up after one try," Sue said. "It's not like you."

"It's not like you to miss a show that was so important to me," I countered. "We still haven't heard from *you*."

"Don't change the subject," Sue retorted. "I'll bet the kids in your group would try it again with just a little push from you. After all, they've done all the work already. Why not do the play?"

"Maybe," I conceded.

"They're just mad at you because it was Corey who ruined everything." Sue paused. "How's Paul?"

"It's been really hard on him," I said. "That is *not* the way he wanted the group to find out. Now he's out and he had to tell his parents. They flipped. His father is threatening to toss him out of the house. It's pretty bad."

"I'm sorry," Corey said, her voice weak. "I'm sorry."

"I think Paul deserves to hear *you* say that," I stated.

"I'll phone him," Corey agreed.

And of course even though Corey was feeling too guilty to mention it, I knew that some of it was my responsibility. After all, I'd told Corey and Sue, hadn't I? But Paul never reproached me—his silence in this case showed more class than a billion words. I was really grateful to him for that and it showed me what a fine person he is. I guess he understood that old rule about being allowed to tell your best friends and he didn't blame me.

"She's sorry," Sue said to me. "How about letting it go?"

I thought for a moment.

"All right," I conceded. "I'll make up with you, Corey. But I never want to see you like that again."

"I never want to see me like that again either," Corey agreed, obviously relieved. "I was sick as a dog after, I can't remember properly. And Mom is insisting I volunteer at the clinic or the hospital for the rest of the summer so I won't get in any more trouble."

"*I* didn't tell her," I said. Although Sue and I might have had to tell Mom eventually—Corey was obviously getting in way too deep.

"I know," Corey replied. "It was Lonnie's dad. Lonnie was so blasted that her dad discovered everything and then phoned all the parents. Anyway, we're not *quite* finished with our 'Telling' are we? Because we still haven't heard from Sue about where she was that afternoon. Wasn't Sue supposed to be at your show?"

Both of us looked at our older sister and waited expectantly.

"I just forgot," she muttered.

"Come on, Sue!" Corey exclaimed. "You made me tell. I don't believe you forgot!"

"Why not? Why couldn't I forget? Am I so perfect I

always remember everything, I always do the right thing? I just forgot!"

"We're not saying you couldn't forget, Sue," I said. "We're saying you didn't. Now *tell!*"

Sue sighed. "Only if you *swear* it'll *never* go further than this room. That means neither of you can even tell your best friend." She paused. "Swear."

"I swear," I said.

"Me too," said Corey.

CHAPTER 11

Sue handed me her latest poem. I read it aloud.

> *"She walked softly through the forest*
> *A tree caught her hair,*
> *gently she tried to free herself,*
> *to no avail.*
> *She tugged harder, with more force,*
> *to no avail.*
> *She struggled and screamed for help,*
> *to no avail.*
> *She accepted her fate,*
> *She was set free.*
> *The tree's name was love."*

"I like it," Corey said.
"So do I," I agreed. "Now tell."

"After we went to bed, the night of our 'Telling,'" Sue began, "I lay awake trying to decide what to do about Mark. The next morning I called him, asked him to come down, and as you both know, invited him to stay here. I figured I'd just tell him the truth when he got here. I knew it would be complicated because of Patti though, so I called her right after I spoke to Mark.

"'What's up?' she said.

"'Well,' I replied, 'Mark called last night and he wants to come down.'

"'Great!' she replied. 'I'll tell Mom.'

"'No, Patti, listen, don't be mad but he's going to stay here.'

"'Why? You've got no room.'

"I took a deep breath then blurted it out fast. 'He told me he wants to stay here.'

"For a minute she didn't say anything. The line sounded dead.

"'Patti?'

"'What?'

"'I didn't try to convince him. He called and asked if he could come down and if he could stay here. Let's not fight over a guy.'

"'I thought he liked me.'

"'I thought he liked us both and he does. It's just that he sees me more romantically than he sees you.'

"'Great.'

"'Sorry.'

"'Oh, you're right. No sense fighting over a guy. Hey, I gotta go.'

"'Sure you aren't mad?'

"'Yeah, sure.'

"And she hung up. I wasn't so sure though. I mean I know she didn't *want* to be mad but that didn't mean she wasn't.

"Anyhow, Mark came down that day. The same day you were convincing everyone to do your play," she said to me. "You were working late with Paul, Mom was on night shift and Corey was out at a party, remember?"

Corey and I nodded.

"So we were kinda on our own. I figured he'd hardly see Mom because, you know, when she's on nights she's either out of the house or sleeping so I relaxed about that. We went out for coffee after he got here then came back and hung out in my room." She paused. "We'd never even kissed before and we kinda got into it that night."

Her cheeks began to get red. "He was just so much sexier than anyone I'd ever been with. Man, I was really . . ."

"Turned on?" Corey suggested.

"Yeah, turned on. And he wasn't pushy at all—it was mutual."

"You've never done anything with anyone," I said. "What happened to all your resolve about waiting till you're older and in a long-term relationship and all that?"

"I didn't stop believing in all that," Sue replied, "I just kinda forgot it. Anyway, you're interrupting. So the next day we hung out together, and went out for dinner, and he only met Mom for a minute. Mind you, she managed to fit in two really filthy jokes."

"You *had* told him, hadn't you?" I quizzed her. "He didn't still think Mom was a doctor did he?"

"Well, actually, it kinda never came up, she was working and we were getting along so well, and you know—no, I hadn't told him."

"Sue!" I admonished her.

"I know, I know. And then remember we drove up to Toronto for a couple days to spend time with his friends and go to the ROM. You were both so busy then, I'm sure you hardly noticed I was gone. I stayed at his house this time and his parents were really nice. At one point his dad asked what Mom did and Mark told him she was a doctor."

"Did you correct him then?"

"Well, no, I was too embarrassed. But I did say, well, she delivered babies and did mostly women's health care."

I sighed.

Sue quoted, "'Oh, what a tangled web we weave when first we practise to deceive.' It was just like that. I couldn't figure a way out. The closer we became the harder it got to come clean and tell the truth.

"Anyhow, we drove back here yesterday, the day of your first performance. I know you'd told me about it on the phone and asked me to be there. Mark was going to come with me, then drive back to Toronto right after so I could take last night and today to get ready for camp. I decided to tell him the truth on the way home in the car.

"The conversation went something like this:

"'Mark, I have something to tell you.'

"'What?'

"'I don't know how to tell you this, but basically we've had a big misunderstanding.'

"'We have?' he said, and he seemed really surprised.

"'Yes.'

"'What?'

"'Well, when we were talking about what my mom does for a living, the first time I was in Toronto at Patti's, you kinda assumed she was a doctor.'

"'So?'

"'So—she's not!'

"'What?'

"'She's not.'

"'Why did you tell me she was?'

"'I didn't. You assumed it.'

"'Why didn't you correct me?'

"I muttered so he could hardly hear me, 'I didn't want to.'

"He seemed incredulous. 'Why not?'

"'Your family is so straight. So . . . well, wealthy. Suddenly I thought you'd think less of me if you knew what my mom really does.'

"'What does she do? Is she a plumber?'

"'No, she's a midwife. A nurse. And she works at a women's clinic.'

"He looked at me and almost drove off the road. 'What's wrong with that?'

"'Nothing,' I grumbled.

"'I don't get it,' he said, bewildered.

"'Look, I've been an idiot. I don't know why I did it. I had a moment of stupidity and then I didn't know how to get out of it. I wasn't really afraid of you hearing about what Mom does. I was worried that when you found out I'd lied, you'd hate me or not trust me or lose all respect for me, and I didn't want that.'

"He grinned at me. 'You're crazy, you know that?'

"'I know.' I paused. 'I'm sorry.'

"'It's all right. We all do stupid things. I'm just sorry you didn't trust me enough to be honest from the start.'

"That made me feel even worse.

"'So am I,' I replied.

"And that was it. We drove in silence the rest of the way. I figured it was probably all over and I felt just sick about it. Anyway, we got home and everyone was out. Mom was at work, you were partying," Sue said to Corey, "and you were at the fair," she said to me.

"'I should start to pack,' I said to Mark, 'before we go to the fair.'

"'Sure,' he agreed. 'Want me to make us some sandwiches?'

"I said that would be nice, showed him where everything was, and came up here to start to organize my stuff. About twenty minutes later he came in with a plate of tuna sandwiches and some juice. He put them on the counter, then he came over to me and held me by the shoulders and looked into my eyes. I completely melted.

"'I'm not mad,' he said. 'I'm crazy about you. I wish you didn't have to go to camp.' And he kissed me. And then—"

Sue paused. We waited. Sue didn't continue. As the silence stretched out both Corey and I looked at each other, as knowledge dawned on us.

"You—" I said, yet I couldn't really believe it.

"You did it!" Corey exploded.

"Were you safe?" I asked.

Sue nodded.

"He just *happened* to have a condom on him," Corey commented. "Right."

"How was it?" I asked, dying to know.

Sue shook her head. "Not great. The kissing and stuff leading up to it was a lot more fun than doing it was. I got nervous, he got nervous, it was just kinda stupid." Sue sighed.

"Why did you do it?" I asked.

"Oh, that's *such* a smart question," Corey snipped. "She was horny, that's why."

"No, it's not!" Sue snapped. "It's not why. That is, yes I was, but why go all the way? I think it's because I was so thankful that he still liked me and I wanted to please him—"

"Nice, nice, she wanted to be nice," Corey said.

"I wanted to please him, I wanted him to still like me, just like when I let him believe Mom was a doctor! What an idiot I am! And all this time I thought I had nothing to prove to anyone!"

I got up, kneeled down by Sue and gave her a big hug. "It's okay," I said. "It's normal to react that way."

Sue began to cry. "What an idiot I am."

"No, you're not," I said, trying to soothe her but secretly half agreeing. "You're not." Still, I couldn't believe Sue, my older sister, the smart one, the mature one, could be so stupid. It kinda scared me.

"You're not an idiot," Corey agreed. "If anyone in this room is an idiot, it's me."

"That's true!" Sue and I replied together, Sue grinning through her tears.

"I called him today," Sue added.

"And?" I asked.

"And I told him I wasn't sorry we'd done it, which is not exactly true, but that I've thought about it and I don't want to do it again. I want to go back to just the kissing stuff."

"And?"

"And he said that was fine with him. That he really likes me and he wants us to be together and we'll have lots of time for that later."

"Wow!" said Corey.

"Cool," I said.

For a moment we sat in silence.

"At least now I know why you weren't there," I said at last.

"But I'll come and see it, I promise," Sue said.

"There's nothing to see," I said, still feeling bitter. "Besides, you leave tomorrow morning."

"You're going to march in there tomorrow and get everyone to agree to do it again," Sue said. "And I'll see it the weekend I get home from camp."

"And I'll come," Corey said. "Alone. Or with some friends who can behave," she added. "If I can get out of the hospital or clinic long enough," she sighed.

I smiled. "All right," I agreed, "I'll try."

"Come on," Sue said, "I have to get to bed. Big day tomorrow." She got up. "Hands." The three of us joined hands. We began to circle, slowly at first.

> *When shall we three meet again*
> *In thunder, lightning, or in rain*
> *When the hurly burly's done,*
> *When the battle's lost and won.*

Over and over we recited our chant, holding on to each other tightly until we snapped away and twirled into our rooms, to sleep, and to get ready for another day.

The next morning, just before she left, Sue gave me this poem:

> *Here I go, Lover, again,*
> *in this nameless night, in this frameless bed,*
> *where my eyes are not blue*
> *and my hair isn't tangled.*
>
> *But I am glowing,*
> *I might be the moon against your skin.*
> *Don't close your eyes too tightly.*
> *I might be gone soon.*

This is where we meet
when we are half-asleep and drowsy.
You barely even kiss me
and when you do it is empty.

You tell me I am pretty,
you say I'm a good girl.
We talk of touching as necessity,
we thank our parents for this world.

We make words like infants, noisy and lazy.
You call me God, I think I'm going crazy
in this night.
Oh how I hate to leave this night!

But the morning is stronger
than any force to make me stay,
or any excuses we could make.
I think I see Dawn. Here I go, Friend, again.

>─◆─○─◆─◄

I guess there were some lessons the three of us learned this summer. Corey, I hope, has learned not to lose herself *completely* in the group. I've learned to work *with* a group. We were on opposite ends, weren't we? Me too independent, her not independent at all. And Sue? She's kept our little group, us three sisters, together through it all, and maybe has learned a bit about who she is. She's got *nothing* to be ashamed of but it's her that has to accept that.

I don't know what will happen tomorrow. This isn't like some novel where everything just stops at the end. Our lives continue. Corey still hasn't given up her friends. I still have to convince everyone to try the play again and muddle through my relationship with Dan, which is totally confusing. Paul has to struggle through every day, and Corey has to live with what she did to him. Sue has to live with a decision she regrets already.

It's funny about stories—how much is true, how much is lies. I mean, when I found out the truth about the witch-burning I thought everyone would be *thrilled* to know. But it looks like people would rather *not* know if it's going to make them have to change. I mean, if women find out the truth about their history, does that mean they have to change now, in the present? Do men have to change too?

And then, there's our little histories. I know we didn't tell each other everything in our "Tellings." I know I left stuff out. I know Sue and Corey held back, didn't tell *everything*. Sometimes on purpose, sometimes just 'cause we weren't thinking about it. And when you learn things, you *might* have to change, right? Like if Lee-Ann told Chelsea that Chelsea's boyfriend had been hitting on her, Chelsea *couldn't* react the same way to her boyfriend, could she? But as long as she doesn't know, life goes on as usual. What's that old saying—"ignorance is bliss."

Well, my story is over. I've told it the best way I could. Did I leave anything out? Definitely! I hardly spoke about Mom at all. That could be a story in itself. I mean, how we've had to cope living without a dad and with a mom who's away a lot—and how she's had to cope. How sometimes I hate her for not being there and how sometimes I realize that we've grown up faster because we've had to. Well, see what I mean? I could go on forever just about Mom if I wanted to, but that's for another story.

There'd be a million different ways to tell this story, too, that's for sure. But what's important to me is that just by trying, things became clearer to me. And through our "Tellings" we all helped each other. I guess for now, that'll have to do.